THE MIDNIGHT CREATURE FEATURE PICTURE SHOW

THE MIDNIGHT CREATURE FEATURE PICTURE SHOW

DAVID C HAYES

Copyright © 2018 by David C Hayes

ISBN **978-0-9988878-6-9**

Cover Illustration by Joshua Werner

Cover Design by Adam Millard

Originally Released by Crowded Quarantine Press in 2015

Published by Dragon's Roost Press 2018

The
Dragon's Roost Press

DEDICATION

This is for Kevin and Jeff.

"Hack" first appeared in *High Stakes* from Evil Jester Press

"That's a Wrap" first appeared in *Canopic Jars* from Great Old Ones Publishing

"That Other Plan from Outer Space" first appeared in *Cannibal Fat Camp* from Thunderstorm Books

"Rode Hard, Put Away Wet" first appeared in *Gruesome Tensome: A Tribute to HG Lewis* from Novello

"Misty Hills of Dreamer Sheep" first appeared in *Desolation* from Dragon's Roost Press

"End Scene" first appeared in *The Dead Rise* from Burning Bulb Publishing

"Savage Sword of King Conrad" first appeared in *Alter Egos* from Source Point Press

Pegged was originally published in a limited edition by Dynatox Ministries

"Model Employee" first appeared on Bizarro.com's Flash Fiction Friday

"The Caprophagus" first appeared in *Bleed for Me: A Literary Tribute to GG Allin* from Weirdpunk Books

Hazmat was originally published by Severed Press

CONTENTS

VAMPIRES!

HACK

The Yuk Yuk Hut on Clark Street in downtown Chicago was dark as pitch when Jeff 'El Jefe' Dolniak entered the front doors. It was long after hours at the upscale comedy club but Jeff didn't know that anything, anywhere, could be this dark. *This joint is Africa-dark*, he thought and, contrary to standard operating procedure, he was too freaked out to laugh at his own joke. He cleared his throat, quietly. There was no response. For a guy that routinely performed in front of hundreds of laughing fans (and whose material was a couple of steps left of just plain wrong), the quiet and the darkness and the, well, creepiness, had really thrown him off. It was worth it, though. At least El Jefe thought it was worth it even if he couldn't exactly explain what it was. Gathering all of his courage, mid-level comedian Jeff Dolniak called out bravely into the darkness.

"Uumm… hello?" he said, "It's, uhh, it's me… Jeff." Nothing. Wait.

"Mr. Dolniak, it is a pleasure to see you," sluiced through the darkness, the words oily and black. The spotlight blazed from the rear of the club lighting up the stage next to Jeff. El Jefe jumped, his heart in his throat. The round spotlight exposed the small stage, stool and microphone. This wasn't Jeff's first time in the club and he knew that a house that seated around 200 fell off into the darkness beyond the light. The Yuk Yuk Hut had been a Chicago institution since before World War II. You played there and you are up for a major tour, that's just how it worked. Well, Jeff knew how it worked for real… at least he thought he did. That was why he was there, scared half to death.

A heartbeat behind the light, Kyle Dillon, the club manager, moved into the cast off glow of the spot. He smiled, like always, and extended his hand. Jeff had never seen Dillon without that smile. It unnerved every comedian that played The Hut and Jeff had always assumed it was a negotiating tactic. Tactic or not, it effectively made any situation awkward. Jeff tentatively took Dillon's hand in a perfunctory shake and moved his hand away quickly. The smile never wavered.

"I'm glad you took Mr. Timponi up on his offer. He sees a great deal in you, Mr. Dolniak. A great deal indeed."

"Thank you. Err, I mean thank Mr. Timponi for me." If possible, Jeff thought that Dillon's smile grew wider and whiter.

"Oh, you'll be able to thank him yourself. Follow me to the dressing area. You will have approximately fifteen minutes to prepare and then you will perform."

With that, Dillon turned and disappeared into the murky shadows of the club. Stumbling after him, Jeff tried to keep up. He had played the club before, during business hours, of course, when the lights were on, so he managed not to kill himself as Dillon walked around tables toward the rear of the establishment. They eventually reached the dressing area and Dillon held the door for Jeff.

"Please, Mr. Dolniak, enter." Jeff, managing a weak smile, entered the small dressing room. A bottle of bourbon, his favorite kind, a tumbler and ice were already there. Jeff felt a little more relaxed seeing his best friend on the table like that. Well, one of his best friends. Like most comedians worth his salt, Jeff ran with Jim, Jack, Johnnie, and Jos´ pretty regularly. Too regularly, if you asked his three ex-wives.

"So, it will just be Mr. Timponi?" Jeff asked. He stammered a bit saying the man's name now that he knew the truth.

"And myself. Here are the ground rules: You are to tell three jokes. These are not to be slice of life pastiches where you wax poetic and make humorous observances about the bizarre, uniquely American condition. You will tell three jokes that have a set-up, a body, and a punch line. Do you understand?"

"Yes," Jeff answered, "I guess, but why can't I just do my set that…"

"Mr. Timponi is a purist and he believes that any individual able to tell a joke will be able to enthrall an audience with a story. It is the joke, though, the bare essence of comedy that is so difficult," Dillon's smile, as always, never wavered. Even as he cut off and chastised Jeff.

"I understand."

"In addition, you are not to curse or use profane language. Mr. Timponi believes that is evidence of a weak mind. You do not want Mr. Timponi to believe you have a weak mind, do you?"

"No."

"Good. You will have three attempts to make Mr. Timponi laugh. Three jokes, three attempts. If you succeed in that endeavor, he will see to it that you, Mr. Dolniak, will have a long and illustrious career as long as you see fit to stay alive. If you do not, well, you're aware of the consequences.

I'll leave you to it." Dillon exited, shutting the door behind him.

Jeff exhaled deeply. He hoped it was at least worth it. He looked into the mirror ringed with small lights, and stared into the eyes of a good, unknown comedian that knew his last shot at something, anything, of value in the industry was right here and right now. If he didn't make it tonight, though… shit. He didn't even want to think about it. Not many people got this opportunity. At least he didn't think many people did. It's not like you'd hear from the guys that blew it.

Jeff opened the bourbon and filled the glass. He ignored the ice and took a long guzzle letting it burn down his throat. He shivered with the smoothness of the drink and took a deep breath. He was really going to do it. Tony Timponi's challenge. A couple of years ago he would have laughed off anyone that brought it up but Jeff knew now. He knew that Tony Timponi was the real fucking deal.

Tony Timponi was the original, and only, owner of The Yuk Yuk Hut, established in 1941. If he had bought the joint at eighteen that would make him 90 years old or so and, after glimpsing Mr. Timponi, Jeff could see that the guy was nowhere near 90. He didn't appear often (although legend has it that Mr. Timponi has seen every comedian that had ever played The Hut) but when he did he looked thirty-five, forty years old. People always said that it's a big Timponi Family joke. The sons and the grandsons just kept taking Mr. Timponi's place and playing him like some cryptic Andy Kaufman rib, but that wasn't it. Tony Timponi was really the same guy and, with the advent of the internet, it was pretty easy to figure out a timeline.

After Dillon approached Jeff after one the shows last week and made THE offer, the one that comedians talk about very quietly over drinks or coke or whatever, Jeff did a little research. Any vaudeville historian worth their salt would tell you that it hit its heyday in the 1920s, but the 'polite company' variety show really came into vogue in the late 1800s. Gentleman song and dance men, zany comedians and screwball clownish performances were the hallmark of the vaudeville review. Most of the shows travelled on a circuit, going from town to town, city to city, like modern medieval minstrels. In the early days of vaudeville, running the Midwest territory, there was one name that drew them all in, the men and women, kids and adults. That was Top Hat Tony Timponi and he was considered the funniest man in Chicago (and surrounding areas). Most people who read that on a poster may have disregarded it as some kind of clever advertising. Barnum-esque publicity, maybe. Anyone who'd seen a Top Hat show knew better. Chances were their sides still hurt from the last time Tony was in town.

Tony played to sold out crowds from Elgin to Detroit, Minnetonka to Des Moines and everywhere in between. He had even started to branch out to the East Coast in the mid-1920s and, with that expansion, got a serious look from the Hollywood studios. Top Hat's patented brand of polite, family friendly, comedy featured some physical work that would put some of the Holly-weird bigwigs (Buster and Charlie, watch out) to shame. His calling card, though, was the joke. He could set it up, make 'em wait for it and then knock it out of the park like no one else. The funny man had a rocket strapped to his back and he was headed straight to the top. Until 1929. After that he disappeared. Just like that, poof. The dates were cancelled and a replacement act was quickly booked to fill the empty slot and the name Top Hat Tony Timponi slowly faded until it was nothing more than a name that fellow comedians would raise a glass to, toasting his genius, as they stole the jokes that Tony obviously had no more use for.

Anthony Timponi, the name, appeared on the requisite documents in the late 1930s to open The Yuk Yuk Hut and it had been there ever since. It was a Chicago institution, along with the Blues and Second City. From the onset, The Hut managed to become a proving ground for young comedians. Anyone that was anyone had played The Hut at some point and, through the years, it became a destination point for comedians and audiences alike. It wasn't until the 1960s, though, that the whispers started. The little stories told in the dark about Tony Timponi, The Hut, and just how hard it was to make it in this business.

Jeff had heard the talk before. Tony Timponi would make the offer of a game to certain comedians… comedians that he felt had merit. If they agreed, those comedians would be in the same place that Jeff was right now. Each of them was given three chances to make a genuine comedy legend laugh. If you succeeded, the sky was the limit. Although no one ever knew for sure, there had been talk regarding just who benefitted from the Timponi Touch. Dangerfield, Kinison (imagine him telling a clean joke), Carlin… all of them genius performers and each of them a certifiable success, artistically and financially. They would never indicate whether or not Tony had a hand in their success, no one would, but one can wonder, right?

And those unlucky stiffs that didn't make the big man laugh? No one ever heard from them again. The funny part was that no one heard of them to begin with so it wasn't like there was a big void in the comedy world by their absence. Another slot just opened up at an open mic; it was as simple as that.

Jeff slugged down another drink and refilled the glass. He had to will himself to not suck that one dry right away. It would do no good to go up there sloshed, that's a quick trip to deads-ville. Jeff laughed. It was that other rumor about

Top Hat Tony Timponi that really disturbed him, especially after his research. When a comedian is doing poorly and the audience is just crickets out there, the performers call them dead. Jeff laughed again. He was pretty sure that his audience tonight was already dead. Well, undead, technically. All the whispering and all the talk about just who Tony Timponi was usually skirted around just what everyone thought Tony Timponi was. Only very late at night, when the bartender gives you an extra couple hours after last call while the staff cleans up, did anyone dare say what everyone already thought.

Vampire.

There, it was out. Jeff had thought the word and could no longer bring it back. If you didn't get Mr. Timponi to laugh then you became lunch. Dillon did not say that verbatim. He did indicate that, if Jeff lost, he should make sure that all his affairs were in order before coming to The Yuk Yuk Hut. Walking through those doors was acceptance of the terms. Why did Top Hat do this? No one knew. Boredom, maybe? Jeff liked to think that Top Hat was just concerned with the quality of his industry. Tony had been around so long he could see all the bumbling oafs come through over the years. The guys that told dirty nursery rhymes or simply smashed watermelons or celebrated the blueness of their collars... the lowest common denominator of comedy had to anger Tony Timponi. He was a master, a classic. He had a PhD in funny and these hacks only managed to tell toilet jokes. That's what Jeff wanted to believe. He was chosen, he had something that Timponi saw and, by God, he was going to give it his best shot. Comedy was his life, literally now that Colleen had left, and he wanted this more than anything else. There was no 'plan b,' like a college degree or a factory job back home. Failure meant death so, in effect, he had nothing to lose.

It was still scary as shit, though. And he *still* hadn't thought through his three jokes when there was a knock at the door.

"Mr. Dolniak?" Dillon asked through the door.

"Yup," Jeff answered, surprised he could even squeak that out. The door opened and the club manager had the same smile plastered across his face.

"You're on." Dillon didn't wait for an answer. He turned and walked toward the front of the club. Taking a deep breath Jeff shot back the last of the bourbon and followed.

Dillon sidestepped to the left as they entered the main show area. Jeff trudged forward, through the murkiness, and aimed right for that spotlight and that stage. He took the steps one by one and felt the weight of the world on each of them. It was all he could do pull himself up the short flight. Once on stage, he moved through molasses getting to the microphone, adjusted it to his height, and cleared his throat. The mic was on and his gurgling phlegm echoed throughout the empty club.

"Oh Jesus!" he said, hearing his bodily fluids all around him. The exclamation was too loud as well. Jeff stood back from the mic quickly and took a deep breath. Dillon's voice slid through the club to the stage.

"Calm down, Mr. Dolniak."

Jeff nodded and took a couple of deep breaths. He made a mental conviction, plastered his 'comedy' smile on and stepped up to the mic on more time.

"Good evening everyone, well, you, Mr. Timponi. My name is Jeff Dolniak, and…"

"He knows that, Mr. Dolniak. Tell your first joke."

Jeff responded by giving in and shutting up. *Jesus Christ*, he thought, *Haven't even said hello and I'm getting heckled. This business is murder!* At the thought, Jeff cracked a smile.

At least he could get *himself* to laugh. His mind working a mile a minute, Jeff started the first joke that came to him.

"Johnny and his wife had fallen on some tough times, this economy, you know what I mean? Johnny can't find a job, his wife can't find a job… but she is quite attractive. So, they concoct this plan where his wife, Evie, would take to the streets. She would become a prostitute and Johnny would play her pimp. They watched a bunch of movies, like *Pretty Woman*, to make sure they were getting it right. So, Johnny sends his wife out on the first night and she comes back smiling from ear to ear. She has had a great night, she tells her husband, and she hands over the loot. It's a hundred and two dollars and fifty seven cents. Johnny can't believe it. Over a hundred bucks! He was curious, though, and asked her, 'Who gave you fifty seven cents?' His wife smiled and said, 'Everybody.'"

Jeff stepped back, waiting. He waited a moment more. Nothing. No chuckle, no laugh. Not even a derisive snort. *Fuck*, he thought. Jeff gave Mr. Timponi another moment… wait for it, wait for it…

"Mr. Dolniak," Dillon shattered the quiet, "You may try again."

One down. Jeff's mind raced. He needed something. Maybe Timponi didn't like the hooker thing. Maybe it was too old? Jeff sweated bullets and licked his lips. They were beginning to dry and crack. His mouth felt like it was filled with cotton. *Dead room, that's for sure*, he thought, and laughed out loud this time. *I slay me*, he thought again and laughed one more time. Not even the image of Tony Timponi swooping in from the rafters, fangs bared, eyes blazing, could spoil it.

"Mr. Dolniak?"

"I'm good. I'm fine. I'm ready." Jeff said, between chuckles. He stepped up to the mic again and took a deep breath. *Jokes. He wants jokes? I'll give him jokes.* He went for broke.

"You know," Jeff started, "Ever since I've been a little kid I have been fascinated with prison. No, seriously, I have. What it takes to get there, what you have to do in prison. I must admit, I had been a bit infatuated with the idea that there was free food, free cable TV, and you got to have a roommate. As an only child, I dug the roommate thing. That particular fringe benefit took on a new meaning as I got older, as did the whole prison thing. I realized what you had to do in order to get to prison and I also realized what people did to you when you were in prison… if you know what I mean. So, I developed a plan. I always thought I would end up there, but I saw how these inmates, theses common criminals were approaching the incarcerated thing all wrong. They worked out and got big and buff so they could beat up any gang rapists that came by, right? Well, not me. I'm going to eat. I'm going to eat and eat and eat. As you can already tell, my derriere is a little larger than most. It's plump. Imagine that even bigger. Much bigger. There is a show on TV called *600 Pound Virgin*. That guy's rear end is smaller than I'm thinking. When all the other tough guys are fighting off the rapists I'm just gonna' let them in. Go right ahead. With an ass that big you'll just be playing in the cheeks anyway. You'd need to be hung like John Holmes to hit my sweetmeat!"

This joke always worked. He had told it across the country. Even Republicans in Kansas were at least ashamed to laugh at this one. It poked fun at all of society's pariahs: fat people, convicts, rapists, comedians… everyone. Jeff waited for that chuckle. Even a hundred-year-old douchebag that had heard every joke on the planet had to laugh at that one. Didn't he? Another moment. Nothing. Jeff threw his hands up in exasperation. He couldn't take it. He was going to die and there was no way out. Screw it.

"One more time, Mr. Dol…"

"Shut up," Jeff cut Dillon off, knowing full well that he was probably signing his own death warrant, "Just shut up. Yeah, I get it. One more joke. Whatever. I don't need some Renfield wannabe with a goofy smile telling me I'm two-thirds dead, ok?" Jeff squinted into the spotlight, trying to make out a shape, anything, in the audience, "And you, Top Hat? Yeah, I know about you. Everyone does they just won't talk about it. You're some kind of comedy Godfather, right? Lives forever, feeds on comics that don't cut it. I get it. You're probably looking up here like I'm lunch. Well, too bad for me, right?" Jeff stood back. He kicked the stool over in frustration and ripped the mic from the mic stand.

"Goddamn vampire, they said. Can't trust him, they said. I'm not talking about you, I'm talking about every other goddamn comedy promoter and club owner on the planet. You, Nosfer-fuckyou, you're the only honest one! You admit it! Know what I hope? I hope all the goddamn villagers get their goddamn torches and they come down here. I don't want them to kill you, though. I want them to tie you down to chair and put a fucking TV in front of you. You won't be able to move and I want them to play all of the fucking *Twilight* movies in a row, over and over again, until you decide to kill yourself. By my estimation, it should be about twenty minutes into the first one."

"Mr. Dolniak!" Dillon shouted from the audience.

"Can it. Go eat a fly or something. I'm almost done anyway. Finally, I just want to thank you for the opportunity and warn you that I'm a borderline alcoholic so what I got in these veins may be a little watered down for your tastes. Anyway, have at it."

Jeff laughed then, long and hard. He knew the end was near so he righted the stool, took a deep breath, and sat down. The spotlight shut off at that point, throwing the club into complete darkness. Before he could even blink and start the eye adjustment process, Jeff felt a presence behind him. It was cold and dark. Hands grasped Jeff's shoulders and he went rigid. The hands had long fingers that were almost gentle at the touch, like when humans 'test' a piece of fruit for freshness. Jeff could barely feel their weight, but he knew they were there. He knew their intent as well.

A cold, dry tongue tasted the vein up the side of Jeff's neck. The sound of the tongue scraping against his five o'clock shadow was like Velcro separating and it made Jeff shiver. He pulled the microphone up one last time.

"They told me that comedy was filled with a bunch of bloodsuckers and that I'd never make it. Guess they were right after all." Jeff let the mic drop to the floor. It landed with a thunk that reverberated through the speaker system. Jeff closed his eyes, preparing for the end. Wait for it. Waaait for it…

The hands left his shoulders and the room warmed up a bit just then. And, from the shadows, Jeff heard the most awful sound on the planet, like nails on a chalkboard underwater. It was music to his ears.

MUMMIES!

THAT'S A WRAP

"Fuck Karloff," he said. It was out there, right in the middle of the room, and he could never take it back.

The *room* was The Actor's Studio in New York and the year was 1964.

The *he* was Lance Polland, an up and coming thespian, who was contemplating changing his name to Lance Rivers because it sounded powerful.

Lance scanned the room, the shocked faces of his fellow Actor's Studio classmates staring back at him, and swallowed hard. It had taken him a long time to get here, not everyone auditioned their way into that exclusive training ground. Making a quick decision, Lance doubled-down on his earlier sentiment. Feeling particularly courageous (since he had just been cast in a new picture), Lance put on his best Brando and sneered.

"As a matter of fact, fuck Chaney, too... and that limey, Lee!" Lance smirked. Usually, that was enough to disarm anyone. His, now official, movie star good looks had carried him through school and social events with ease. He was charming, square-jawed, and blonde. Just a hair over six feet tall with a body that harkened back twenty years to a savage Johnny Weismuller, Lance was used to getting away with saying just about anything.

Not in here, not in the Studio. To make matters worse, he just shit on Hollywood royalty… and the British guy. The room was aghast.

Nicholson stepped forward, fists balled. He had just finished a picture for Corman with the ailing Boris Karloff and respected the man immensely, even if the rest of the country had forgotten about him. Newman and the skinny kid, Pacino, each grabbed an arm before Nicholson's patented temper vested itself in Lance.

"How the fuck can you say that," Nicholson growled. "You ain't half the actor that Karloff is… and Chaney? He's a fucking *legacy*, you mother…"

No one thought to restrain Fonda. She marched up to Lance, tears streaming from her eyes, and slapped him across the face, hard.

Shocked, Lance recoiled and turned toward her. His eyes blazed. He may have been in the Big Apple just then, but he was Mississippi born and bred and that doesn't get work-shopped out like a drawl does. He stepped forward ready to put a woman in her place.

To her credit, and probably due to genetics, she held her ground. Pacino and Newman were ready to unleash Nicholson on Lance, the other members of the Studio stood against Lance, unified. It looked grim. Lance's only saving grace was that Keitel wasn't there that day.

Strasberg stepped forward. He had been watching from the corner of the room, seeing just how this was going to play out. First and foremost, even above an actor, Strasberg was a behaviorist. Understanding how and why people behaved in the manners that they did was absolutely essential to understand the cause and effect of the human condition.

That understanding was needed to replicate the human condition honestly on stage, screen, etc. He had studied the acting techniques of Konstantin Stanislavski, the Russian genius, and had taken over the artistic directorship of the Actor's Studio in 1951 based on what he called The Method.

Studying under Strasberg was akin to learning strategy from Sun Tzu. The Method required the actor to dispel the memory, context, and emotions of their normal, every-day life. It forced the actor to adopt, physically, mentally, and emotionally, the role that he or she was playing as reality. It was a painful process. One of Strasberg's students, who couldn't handle the process, incidentally, had said that with Lee, one gets an idea of just how painful birth is. Strasberg chuckled when he heard that and quipped, "Birth is painful, rebirth is excruciating." There were people in the room, so all of his subsequent denials fell on deaf ears. Strasberg was right, though, The Method exacted a great price from its practitioners.

In that vein, the master of the The Method commanded a healthy dose of respect, so when he stepped between Fonda and Lance, both of them shook off their anger and backed up. Pacino and Newman let go of a suddenly-calm Nicholson and Burstyn put down the telephone in the studio where she was trying to get through to Keitel's answering service.

Lee was a quiet man, normally, and this was no exception. He was a master, he didn't need tricks and gimmicks to convey any emotion, he simply embodied it. Strasberg turned that intensity onto Lance.

"What did you say, Lance?" Strasberg asked.

Lance stuttered and sputtered. "It was just a joke, Lee. I mean, I wasn't seri.."

"What did you say?"

Lance took a deep breath and then, as quickly as he

could, said, "I said fuck Karloff and Chaney and Lee... not you! The British guy, from that Hammer outfit."

The rest of the room hid smiles as effectively as they could. Lance shifted from one foot to another, nervous. Strasberg had that effect when he wanted to.

"Fuck Karloff... hmmm," Lee said. "Intriguing proposition, but I don't think the old chap would much enjoy that."

The room exploded in laughter. The tension was diffused and Lance, quite noticeably, relaxed.

Lee turned to the other students, exhorting them to resume their exercises, and took Lance by the arm. He led the young actor back to the office.

Strasberg sat Lance down in a desk chair and then took a spot on the edge of the cluttered desk. The teacher folded his arms and looked at Lance, assessing the young man.

Lance withered under that gaze and Lee held it for quite some time before speaking.

"I understand you booked a job today, Lance," Lee began.

"Yes sir."

"And, based on the vitriol in the studio and your chosen targets, I assume you are to be performing in some sort of horror film?"

Lance nodded. "Yes sir. A mummy movie."

"Of course. Tell me about it."

Lance brightened there. This was familiar subject matter... himself. "I am going to play Seti the Fourth, raised from the dead after two thousand years to claim his lost love!"

Strasberg nodded. "And, so, you effectively shit on legendary performers, although we'll have to wait and see about that British guy, because you were really, really excited about playing a mummy. And you did that in front of the class."

Lance's excitement plummeted. He shrank in the chair and had problems making eye contact with Lee. "Uuuh. Yeah…" he said.

Lee nodded. "You did the one thing I ask everyone not to do here. I need all of you, every time you walk in, to leave that Hollywood bullshit at the door, right?"

Lance nodded.

"So what did you do? You not only brought that Hollywood bullshit in here, you flaunted it around like some goddamn Vaudeville act." Lee didn't raise his voice, he never had to.

"I'm so sorry, Lee," Lance managed to squeak out as he started at his shoes.

Strasberg took a deep breath. He looked at the cluttered desk and pushed some papers away to uncover a Rolodex. He flipped through it, eventually landing on the name he was looking for. Snatching the card out, Lee handed it to Lance.

"Ramses Egyptian Catering," Lance read aloud.

"I want you to do well, Lance, I really do, so you'll need to do some homework. What's the name of the picture?"

"*Curse of the Mummy's Shroud*. That makes me the title character, right?"

Lee cringed at the title but recovered in time to nod. "Yep, sure does. For this particular role, Lance, I don't think we can help you very much here, at the Studio."

"Why not?"

"This is The Method, son. Becoming the role. That name and address I gave you is for just that. Ramses runs an Egyptian Catering service, true, but he is also well-versed in what that crazy Russian brought over here and realizes what we need for The Method and is a certified expert on Ancient Egypt. I want you to see him."

Lee looked down at the card and then back at the Rolodex. "What else do you have in there?"

"Everything, Lance. The whole world. That's my job."

Lance nodded and slipped the card in his pocket. "Should I get back out with the others?"

"Not this time, Lance," Lee said. He helped the young man to his feet, pushing him toward the back entrance. "You need to get your head straight with this mummy picture, so look up Ramses today. Head out the back way, you know how Nicholson gets."

"I sure do." Lance whistled his way out of the Actor's Studio into the muggy New York air.

   ***

Lance looked around, cautiously. It was nearing dusk and he had taken two trains, with two bus transfers, to get to the ass end of Queens. He walked down a lonely sidewalk with a summer breeze like dog breath blasting him in the face. Lance stopped and fished the paper out of his pocket again and read it. It hadn't changed: 45367 Pyramid Drive.

Lance lifted his head and looked up and down the sidewalk. There were tenement buildings, three story walk ups, basement apartments, but nothing that could be confused for a catering company. He looked at the building numbers. 45361, 45353, 45365… and there it was.

Lance swore he had looked up and down this street a thousand times since the last bus transfer but now, just as the sun dipped below the urban skyline, he found a little store-front. The sign read: Ramses Egyptian Ca ring. The t and e must have fallen off at some point. The window was cloudy, but Lance could definitely see a light on inside. He reached for the handle and pushed.

The door opened, tinkling a small bell as Lance entered. He was hit immediately with the coolness of the room. It was dry, too. He looked around the area and, contrary to his previous trepidations, it looked like a small, ethnic grocery and catering shop, apparently.

Lance craned his neck to see a counter at the rear of the store.

"Hello?" he called out.

"Enter," a deep, thickly-accented voice returned.

Smiling, in part due to the new climate (air conditioning was incredibly rare in this particular borough) and the successful navigation of the tough, New York streets. If the boys back in Missoula could see him now!

Lance wended his way through the store. The shelves were filled with bottles, carafes and odd, slender jars. There was funny writing on all of them and pictures like he saw in National Geographic on others. Nothing was labeled in English and Lance figured, rightly so, that anyone that couldn't speak Egyptian, or whatever this was, wouldn't have a need for it anyway.

Passing the rows of bottles leaves, spices, homeopathic remedies and odd foods, Lance finally made it to the rear of the store where Ramses waited for him. As Lance approached, the small, dark man looked up.

He was approximately five feet tall and all of, nearly, 110 pounds. He was dark with a large, hooked nose that nestled itself over a bushy, black mustache with salty flecks of white throughout. He smiled at Lance, baring two rows of brown, stained teeth. His gums nearly matched the color of his suit jacket which reminded Lance of fried okra.

Lance extended his hand. "Hello, sir. My name is Lance... uhh... Rivers and Lee Strasberg sent me over."

Ramses stared at Lance's hand until the actor pulled it away, awkwardly. "I am Ramses. You have come to learn, I know?"

Lance nodded. He thought he knew what was happening here. "Yes sir! I am playing Seti the Fourth in *Curse of the Mummy's Shroud*, shooting right here in New York!"

Ramses shuddered at the mention of the title, hiding it less effectively than Strasberg did.

"And I'm real eager to learn as much as I can," Lance continued. "This could be my big break."

Ramses nodded. "Big break, certainly. There are many people that desecrate the values of others to shock or scare an audience. What did you say the name of your mummy was?"

"Seti. The fourth."

"The fourth," Ramses said to himself. He turned then, and shuffled toward the rear of the store. "I thought Ihmotep was bad enough."

Lance just watched the strange little man go until Ramses turned to look at him.

"Well, you are coming?" Ramses asked.

Lance jumped and scooted behind the counter. "On my way. Do you want me to shut the door or lock it or something?"

Without turning back, Ramses parted a beaded curtain and entered the rear of the store. "Taken care of," he said.

Lance stole a glance up the aisle and he'd be damned! The door was closed and locked from the inside.

"Hey! How did you lock the door?" Lance asked.

Ramses called out from the dark beyond the bearded curtain. "Come!"

Biting his lower lip, Lance entered the gloom.

He could see that the room was lit with candles, but the stark difference between the overhead lights of the store and this back area had his pupils growing, trying to compensate. As he adjusted, Ramses voice floated from the ether.

"How long before the shooting of your film?"

"About three months."

Ramses chuckled. "Good."

Lance's vision had just acclimated to the dimly lit room when he noticed a large stone slab, like some kind of weird bed, in the middle of the small area. Three large jars, with the heads of birds for lids, stood along one wall and two sconces, each containing a flickering candle, illuminated the room. Ramses was nowhere in sight.

"Wow, this is groovy, Ramses! I should tell the producer about this place. I bet they could shoot here and you'd get a location fee or someth…"

Ramses brought the truncheon down across the back of Lance's head silently and swiftly. The small, but deadly, club smacked into Lance's head with a crack and the good-looking oaf crumbled to the floor.

Ramses stood over the young man and chuckled. "End scene."

***

Lance blinked his eyes. His head ached and, when he squinted, he thought he could see a cheap, water-stained drop ceiling. This wasn't his apartment. He turned his head, but even a simple motion caused lights to explode in his eyes and a shot of paint to shoot down and back up his spine, nestling right behind his ears and burning.

"What the hell…" he managed to groan out.

"Good, you are awake," Ramses said.

Fighting the pain, Lance turned his head to see Ramses, dressed in some kind of costume, approach him. It took Lance a moment to realize that he was in the back room and on the concrete slab. He tried to raise his arm or sit up but also realized that he was tied down.

"Uuh, Ramses, man. What's going on?"

"You are training for your big film. You are of The Method, no?"

Lance tried his arms again, but they were bound at the wrist, to the table, with leather thongs. "Yeah… yeah, but what is this horse shit? Y'all playing some kind of joke on me?"

Ramses chuckled and reached under his tunic. He pulled a vial of salt from some hidden pouch, and sprinkled pinches of it across the length of Lance's body. "Funny, you see? When you lose concentration, lose the moment of the character, your old voice slips in."

Lance struggled against his binds, the leather rubbing into his wrists and ankles. "I don't know what in tarnation you're talkin' about, old man, but if you don't untie me there is a Sphinx-sized ass whoopin' in your future!"

"Listen to the voice coming out of you. The moment is gone. All the work of learning a new way to talk has been lost." Ramses finished salting Lance's body. He stood stock still and mumbled something under his breath.

Lance struggled underneath the mumbling/chanting/incantation. He lifted his head and, seeing that he was naked, could only think of what was going to be rammed up his ass in the next few minutes. He had experienced the casting couch before, but the casting slab was something completely different.

Ramses stopped chanting and smiled. He looked down at Lance.

"Who is the producing of the film?"

"What? Let me go, man! I won't say anything!"

"Who is the producing of the film?"

"You want a part, right? This is some weird audition thing so I can tell Friedman about it. I get it, man. Look, let me go and I will talk you up to those boys like y'er the goddamn god of acting. Cool?"

Ramses laughed, long and hard. His greasy black mustache bent around the yellow-toothed smile making the entire visage look like some cautionary tale hieroglyphic in the gloom. "I will call Mr. Freidman when we finish. Ready for the close up, you will be!"

Ramses laughed again and pulled a long, metal rod from, possibly, the same region under the tunic where he stored the salt. It was 24 inches long and had a wave near the end before turning at 120 degrees and forming a hook. It was polished, possibly stainless steel, and glimmered in the firelight.

Lance's eyes opened wide in terror. "Oh, sweet Jesus, Ramses! Please don't shove that thing in my ass!"

Ramses shot Lance a look of utter disgust, his lip curling back over diseased gums. "I am not some kind of the sex pervert!"

Lance relaxed a bit, "Thank God, man. What the hell are you going to do, then?"

"The Method! You will be a fine actor of the screen. The finest to ever be a sacred mummy!"

"That metal thing will do it?"

"No, this is for removing the brain before the process of mummification can begin. You will be legend!"

Lance's mouth dropped open as Ramses bent over him. The little Egyptian man nestled the business end of the hook in Lance's left nostril.

"Very simple. The brain is removed with this. Then, organs are removed and cleaned. Each of those jars will hold the dried lungs, intestines, stomach and liver so you may claim them again. Exciting, no?" Ramses took a deep breath, preparing to ram the hook into Lance's skull and extract his brain, bit by bit, though his nostrils.

"Wait! Just wait a minute! Seriously, Ramses, the joke is over, all right? Did Nicholson put you up to this?"

Ramses shook his head. "This is your training, Lance. Your body will be rinsed out with finest wines and your heart... your heart will be placed back inside so you may perform! The finest linens will fill your chest after 40 days. These will give shape to the role, letting you show the audience the pain of Seti, but knowing that his heart belongs to his princess as it rests on down. A metaphor!"

Lance whimpered. "I didn't want this."

"Of course you did. After 70 days I will wrap you in the finest muslin. You will then be ready. You will be a star!"

Lance sobbed and stopped fighting. He accepted the inevitability. "Is this gonna hurt?"

"Only a little," Ramses said and then rammed the hook into Lance's nose.

Lance squealed for a moment, a high-pitched cry that, under other circumstances, may have been called nasally. He convulsed, his body flopping against the concrete, as Ramses worked the hook in and out of Lance's brain pan.

After the first few thrusts Lance had undergone an impromptu frontal lobotomy resulting in fewer convulsions and less overall motor activity. He was dead, officially, before Ramses could even get a third of the brain out.

This was the process that Ramses hated the most. It took so long. Such a useless organ, too. Always getting people in such trouble.

Ramses looked at Lance's vacant eyes, staring up at the ceiling. "Fuck Karloff, indeed. Hmmph. Karloff played at monster… you will become one!"

The little man returned to his work.

***

Fred Freidman, schlock producer, walked into the temporary production office of Shroud Pictures shaking his head.

Leon Kassinger, the director of *Curse of the Mummy's Shroud*, looked up at the producer's entrance, taking a welcome break from going over script rewrites on this, his latest opus. "What's up, Freddy?"

"I don't believe this shit."

Leon's shoulders slumped. "We lost the funding, didn't we?"

Freddy smiled and shook his head. "No. For once, things are looking our way!"

"How so?"

"You know that hillbilly we cast as Seti? The tall guy that walked real stiff in the audition?"

"Yeah," Leon said. "Lance something or other."

"Lance Boil, whatever his name is. His new agent just called and said that since the kid is into this acting bullshit, he will be, at no cost to us, providing his own craft service, transportation and special effects tech in order to stay in character. You believe that shit?"

"Wow. He's making SAG minimum on this picture! That dumb kid is going to lose money!"

Freddy smiled and pulled a half-smoked cigar from his jacket pocket, lighting it with flourish. "That's fine with me, just as long as this picture doesn't lose any money."

Leon and Freddy laughed and laughed. What these kids wouldn't do to make it in the movies.

ALIENS!

THAT OTHER PLAN FROM OUTER SPACE

The Pabst Blue Ribbon cans, nearly a case of them, rattled out of the cab of the truck when Randy opened the door to his 1982 F-150. The hinges creaked, giving the empty cans a little rhythm section to play off of. He chuckled and then lurched out of the truck himself. It was a good day. He got a job. Well, kind of a good day. Ever since the insurance company determined that Randy was goldbricking, faking an injury, and exploiting the workman's comp and disability pay, they had kicked him to the curb like some kind of criminal.

He wasn't a criminal, though. He had a legitimate injury and figured that a big company like McDonalds could afford to pay for a little bed rest. It just got too easy. Days of playing Madden led into weeks of playing Madden, drinking Pabst and looking at BBW porn on the internet. He got sucked into the lifestyle and maintained that pain from his back injury wouldn't allow him to work. The state, and the insurance company, kept him in rent/Pabst money and, as far as he was concerned, this was fine living indeed.

It was the goddamn heat lamp for the burgers that

started the whole mess. Somehow, one of those idiot kids (Randy was 38) that worked with him must have bumped into the lamp. The lamp shifted and pointed directly at a patch of congealed grease on the floor. The heat from the lamp softened the grease and, boom, Randy went ass over heels and hit the floor hard. He was out cold, had a mild concussion and slipped a disc. A full thirty-six months later he was still on disability when he made a tragic mistake.

Randy liked the big girls. Always had. That was one of the reasons that he worked at Mickey D's (that and blowing off his entire senior year of high school and not seeing any merit in a GED since he wasn't going to be a college boy anyway because college boys were sissies and everyone knows that sissies get their asses kicked all the time... but that is a different story). The BBW, big beautiful women, frequented the restaurant regularly and Randy got his fill of eye candy. Big, overstuffed bags of eye candy. Like five pounds of candy in a sack that holds three. He was loving it. Better yet, Randy never spent a dime on food, eating the end of shift morsels meant for the garbage bin. If he did say so himself, he was living the sweet life. Until the accident and the Xbox addiction. Not being at the arches meant he didn't get to see what he called his "bubble babies," though, and that was a bit rough for him.

Randy reached into the cab of the truck and pulled out one of the last full Pabst Blues. He cracked it open and toasted the sky. Randy took a swig and then pulled the little piece of paper out of his pocket that served as the directions to his new job. He was sure that he followed them explicitly, but, as he gazed around the area, it didn't look like anything more than an abandoned field next to a broken down barn. And, for that matter, what kind of construction job started at 9pm? Randy shrugged and sloshed a little more of that hoppy goodness down his throat. He didn't care. If the job started that late, they should expect him to be a little lubed up.

He held the piece of paper up in the moonlight to read it. Luckily for him, none of the words had more than three syllables so he could sound it out pretty good.

"Root 33. Corn feel-d. Lite Con-struc-shon. 9 pm," he said. Nodding, Randy stuffed the paper back in his pocket and waited. Even though he missed his Madden, he smiled. The light of his life appeared one day, right out of the blue, and she was the reason he was even working right now. She was also the reason he got busted.

Even though he wasn't working, Randy still had enough friends that he could get a free meal or two at the arches whenever he needed one. This was most of the time. During one of his last visits, he managed to catch the eye of one of the largest, and loveliest, ladies he had ever seen. Her pouty lips were wrapped around a Big Mac and, if he weren't wearing a back brace (constructed out of an old weightlifting belt and orange suspenders he found at the Salvation Army) he would have slid up to that mama and swept her off her feet. He could only stare as special sauce dripped from the corner of her mouth and she expertly caught it with a plump index finger before it hit the ground, wasted.

Randy grinned, hard and wide, and, much to his amazement, that grin was returned. Not even the poppy seeds in her teeth could turn Randy away. He had to get to know her! Randy shambled, dragging one leg (he assumed that is how injured people walked), up to the young woman. He flattened his mullet down in the back and hitched his pants up as he moved, desperate to make a good first impression. The closer he got, the more beautiful she became.

Her hair was raven black and curled around her plump face. Her alabaster skin was perfect with no discernible joints to mar the curves. Her eyes were gold, truly, gold and the rose red of her cheeks the perfect shade of strawberry-kissed red. Large breasts draped over a larger belly and nothing was left to the imagination. She sported a Whitesnake t-shirt from the 1989 tour, three sizes too small, and poured herself into a pair of Daisy Dukes that morning just for Randy's benefit, he thought.

Randy's rebel flag was already at half-mast when he shuffled up to the table just in time to see the voluptuous vixen shove the last of her Big Mac into her mouth using a Chicken McNugget. Randy nearly lost it, right then and right there.

"Hey," he said, trying to sound smooth as silk, even with the back brace on, "my name's Randy, what's yours?"

She smiled and shoved another lump of processed chicken into her mouth.

"I get it, baby, I get it. Taking it slow. Can I buy you an apple pie?"

She raised an eyebrow, followed by another nugget.

Randy chuckled, "Oh, don't worry about me, I got cash! I'm on disability..." He licked his lips, letting disability roll right off. He needed her to know that he was top of the food chain. Steady income, no bullshit.

She smiled and nodded. From that point forward, it seemed like they were inseparable.

Randy wasn't concerned when he did all the talking, he actually liked to hear himself. He didn't care that, aside from a few grunts and groans, Elsie (that was her name) only communicated via a notepad in short, simple sentences. Randy actually liked that. She was perfect for him: quiet, devoted, and a beast in the sack.

The sex was great, from what Randy could remember. Every time he got a head of steam going, Elsie would drop down, south of the border, and stuff just went crazy. After a minute or two, his eyes would roll into the back of his head and he'd wake up an hour later feeling like a dried leaf. Wow.

They went everywhere together and it was in trying to impress Elsie that he got booted off of the disability rolls. Randy knew a guy that owned a mini golf outfit on Route 8 and both of them were proponents of the barter system. Randy slid the owner of "Nutter Putter" a Filet-O-Fish once a day for about a month, under the table, and Randy could come and go, playing putt putt, as much as he desired. He took Elsie there and, in the middle of showing off (making a particular difficult bank shot through a cardboard hockey goalie, up over a hill, and down a waterfall for a hole in one) he didn't notice his former manager from the restaurant playing two holes back. Davey Anderson, the twenty-some-thing snot-nosed punk general manager of McDonald's #453 from Creek Craw, Michigan, had suspected that Randy was faking and, after a quick video taken from his iPhone, he could prove it.

'Nuff said. Randy was on the street, McDonalds and the insurance company decided not to press charges and, just like that, he was broke. Elsie swooped in to save the day.

Using her little notebook, and wrapping those exquisitely chubby fingers around a pen, she wrote the directions that Randy squinted to read in the moonlight moments ago. She assured him, in her own special 'down south' way, that she had his best interests at heart and that was enough for Randy.

Randy looked around the empty field, made out the husk of a burnt out barn in the growing gloom, and drained the last of his next to last can of Pabst. He thought that this may turn into a long evening when the sky erupted in light.

Brighter than anything he had ever seen before, an intense white light washed over Randy and the immediate area. He fell to the ground, arm over his eyes trying to keep his retinas from burning out, and cowered. A noise, like being behind a fighter jet taking off, blasted the immediate area followed by… something. It was brutal and strong, but Randy couldn't call it wind. It was just a force. A force that flattened him out on the ground, arms and legs splayed out as if her were about to make dirt angels. He couldn't make a sound, either, even if he had something to say.

Although the force pinned him to the ground, paralyzing him, he had no trouble breathing. The intense light beamed onto him from something that hovered above was warm and it felt to Randy like the light was looking *inside* his body. He imagined an x-ray would feel like this, if it felt like anything. The noise blanketed the immediate area and Randy couldn't even hear himself think.

Then, Randy's body was lifted off of the ground. He tried to move his head from side to side, to no avail, and could only manage to strain his eyeballs as far right and as far left as possible to get some kind of gauge in regard to where he was going. As far as Randy could tell, he was going straight up, into the light. His peripheral vision caught a glimpse of some trees, telling him he as at least twenty feet high at that point. Then, the landmarks stopped and it was all sky and stars and moon.

And dark. The light winked out as Randy entered darkness. It looked like an inky black spot in the middle of the sky, like someone had just erased part of the stars. Randy, still immobile, slipped in there. Tears welled in the corners of his eyes and he thought of poor Elsie. What would she do without him?

***

Elsie stepped out of the wooded shadows and watched as Randy slipped into the floating Ink Pod. She smiled. Randy must have passed the initial scan or the Pod would never have accepted him. He'll be nice and cozy for his trip into orbit and the rendezvous with the Colony.

Elsie blinked twice and stood, hands akimbo, staring straight forward after Randy left. If anyone had been around, they could have sworn she was frozen there, in place. Nothing twitched, nothing moved. After a few more moments, Elsie hissed. Not like a snake, or a sparkly vampire, but as if the pneumatic brakes on a school bus had just been released. And then she split in half.

The two sides of Elsie split, right down the middle, and shuttered back like metallic theatre curtains to reveal two small, green men. If they were human, which they were not, they would have looked incredibly old. Septuagenarians at the very least, but tiny (no more than twelve to fourteen inches tall) and green. Within Elsie, the two little men sat in two little captain's chairs, one on top of the other in separate compartments. Each of them had a joystick-like controller rising up between their legs that looked to be how they controlled Elsie from the inside out.

Both of them sucked in a lungful of fresh, non-Elsie air, and exhaled loudly. A perfunctory high-five followed. The man on the bottom stretched his arms and yawned while the man on top pulled a headset microphone out from the arm of the chair and sat it on his head. The little man on the bottom spoke first in a voice that belonged on a Disney rodent.

"I never thought we'd get him out here... this guy was tough!"

"What are you talking about," the man on top answered, "you didn't have to deal with, what did he call it?"

"Sexy time."

"Yeah," the man on top nearly spat out. He shivered from the memory.

"You calling him in? After this one, we should get a bonus."

"Definitely. This BBW Model 9000 Abductee Attraction Unit is the best idea you've ever had! Slim pickings there for quite some time. If we didn't get a subject soon, I'm not sure the mother ship would have renewed our contract."

"Tell me about it. We haven't had any good test subjects since the humans invented basic cable channels. Even the… crap. I always forget what they call them…"

"Rednecks? Hillbillies?" The man on top offered.

"Yeah! Even they were getting wise. Can't break the cardinal rule!"

"Only abduct humans that have no credibility. Recruitment 101!"

Both the man on top and the man on bottom laughed. Then, realizing their work wasn't completely done, they sighed.

"Call it in," the man on the bottom said.

"On it," the man on the top returned.

"Oh, and make sure they set the anal probe to stun.

"Isn't it always?"

GIRL GANGS!

RODE HARD, PUT AWAY WET

August 1968

Tammi Simmons exited the small canvas tent that she shared with Tommy. She stretched, raising her arms to the morning sun, feeling the heat caress her exposed nipples and dry the dribble of Tommy's semen that remained on Tammi's thigh. She smiled, feeling whole and content. Filled with love of life and Tommy, she could barely remember a time when she wasn't fulfilled, spiritually and physically. It was there, though, pushed back to the farthest recesses of her mind. There was darkness long before she joined the Raw Life Nudist Colony but it was nearly forgotten.

Tammi teetered on the precipice of memory, threatening to fall into the abyss of a checkered past, when Tommy exited the tent, grabbing her from behind and rained kisses down on the back of her neck. Tammi giggled but didn't stop him.

Tommy was tall and fit. His shaggy brown hair was evidence of the current trends and his tanned body, sans tan line, was equivocal to Ancient Greek statuary. According to Tammi, as well as many of the young women (and men) at

Raw Life, he was an Adonis. Well over six feet tall, the consummate athlete, sparkling blue eyes and a gentle lover, Tommy was the answer to Tammi's dreams.

Tommy caressed Tammi's large breasts, pressing his ample penis into the small of her back, she could feel it stir one more time. Tammi spun, whipping the long mane of blonde hair around, to face Tommy. They met in a passionate kiss and, without a word, retreated back into the tent. Nothing could intrude on Tammi's bliss, right now.

One hundred miles south, though, that inevitable intrusion straddled a Harley Davidson.

***

Mama Turk perched atop her steel behemoth as it idled outside a small, roadside convenience store. Standing just over five feet tall, and sporting a few extra pounds, the red-headed biker didn't appear physically imposing. When she rode through a town or hamlet, especially those sleepy little places that had never seen a real bike gang, she was down-right scary, though. Mama smiled at the thought of the last town that shook to the ground when her gang passed through. Un-muffled exhaust belched throughout the little hamlet and the squares were afraid to open their doors. Because of Mama Turk's girls. Her gang. She was their Mama and they would follow her to the end of the Earth and back again. Mama's girls were loyal, except one. That was the whole reason for their trip out west. No one left the gang. No one. Mama frowned at the thought as she waited for her girls to finish up inside the store. Not even the gentle vibrations of the motorcycle, usually keeping Mama in a permanent state of sexual excitation, could keep her happy.

The back of her denim jacket was emblazoned with a large logo of two pieces of steel, bladed, and joined in the middle with fire engulfing the metal. "Scissor Sisters" emblazoned the top of the jacket announced the name of the group and every member sported a similar uniform.

Mama didn't have to wait much longer as six women, guns blazing, poured out of the small convenience store. The desert ran miles in each direction and this particular stretch of Route 66 didn't really have much in the way of population, so after a long ride, Mama knew the girls needed a break from the road and a chance to blow off some steam.

She smiled wide, prideful of her little brood of miscreants. The tall, leggy brunette, Sideshow (due to her abnormally long tongue) dragged the young male clerk out through the front doors. His hands were bound and his eyes were wide and filled with terror. If he played his cards right, he may live through this.

Sideshow was followed by the blonde-haired, green-eyed bombshell they called Centerfold; the Hispanic hand grenade named Diabla; the near six and half foot, brooding Swedish monster, Inga; the mousy, but deadly, Half-Pint sporting a crew cut and, finally, Mama's second in command, the recently promoted Vixen. No one was sure exactly what Vixen's heritage was, but she was dark and dangerous.

"Put that pussy, down, Sideshow!" Vixen called out.

Sideshow complied instantly, throwing the clerk to the dirt in a cloud. He coughed and hacked, holding his side, as the gang circled him and laughed.

"Mama!" Vixen yelled to her mentor.

Mama smiled. She wasn't sure how the girls were going to react to Vixen getting the nod. After Raz bolted, Mama was left in a lurch. No one had ever ran away before... ever. It was difficult reigning the girls back in and deciding to give Vixen the spot didn't help, at first. She was mysterious, and the other women didn't know too much about her, but that little bit of fear was a motivator. It took some time, but the old gang was moving forward again. They had a mission, this time, and were hell-bent on revenge.

Mama shook her head, clearing it of Raz and the mission. There was the little matter to be taken care of squirming in the dirty parking lot. She slid off the bike and shut it down, her heels kicking up dust. She spit into the dirt, watching the phlegm being swallowed up by the desert and smirked again. Good leadership to let the girls blow off some steam now and again. Getting wet and wild for a bit never hurt anyone.

The circle of Sisters broke to let Mama in. She straddled the clerk and he stared up at her, terrified.

"Take it out," Mama said.

"Hunh?" was all he could manage.

"Yer pecker, dumb shit. Take it out."

"Excuse me?"

That was all Mama could stand, she didn't like repeating herself. She waved to the girls and they dove in, on each taking a limb. Vixen stepped on the clerk's forehead as he whimpered.

Mama squatted and pulled out her large buck knife. She sliced a large hole out of the clerk's overalls to reveal his manhood. She grinned. A little above average... good. She looked up at the young man's face and guessed him to be around nineteen. Still good. He may manage a few in a row.

Mama reached down and grabbed the poor kid's dick after spitting another wad of phlegm into her hand. As the mucus and calluses touched his genitals, the clerk whimpered. Mama laughed as she stroked him, getting ready for the main event.

"Don't worry, son. You only gotta get all seven of us off and you'll live to see tomorrow."

The kid wailed, but friction, physics and blood flow would never let Mama down and, at least once, he rose to the occasion. Still excited from the idling bike, Mama stood and squatted over the young man.

"Mama always comes first," she said as she lowered herself down.

***

Tammi joined her fellow nudists for breakfast and a meeting of the Raw Council, the group that led the ragtag bunch of naturalists that numbered around 20 to 30 at any given moment. The 'village' was, really, a centralized cabin for meals, social events, etc. and a series of tents, teepees and lean-tos that allowed the practitioners of the naked life to be closer to nature. The Raw Council planned events, voted on memberships and, in all reality, served as role models to the members of the colony. They accepted everyone, of course, and always had.

Two of the founding members, Gladys and Archie Wells, functioned as defacto president and vice president (they had been married so long, they could never agree on who was which). In their mid-sixties, they had lived the natural, nudist lifestyle for years, often being arrested or beaten by conservative rednecks in the early years. Archie had made some wise investments, back in the 'pants and torture' days, as he called them, and had purchased the acreage that housed the colony a few years ago. Gladys proudly only had one outfit, a dress and a pair of shoes, if she ever had to go into town for anything.

Tammi was a member of the council, unanimously elected in the past week due to her service to the colony and, in no small measure, due to her union with Tommy Lawrence. An ex-football player from Stanford, Tommy was popular, charismatic and just the type of leader that Archie could see passing the colony to when it was time.

Rounding out the council was Martin Overbeek, the accountant who had given up material wealth for a freer way of life (which did not include giving up on pumpkin pie resulting in quite a few extra pounds) and Latoria Scott, the chef and nutritionist that kept tabs on the content of the colony's food and the number of pumpkin pies that Martin managed to smuggle in.

They really were a close knit group, a family.

Tammi looked around to each of them, beaming inside to be part of something so wholesome and good. She had a feeling, though. A feeling that she hadn't felt in a very long time. The darkness was coming, heading her way. She was sure of it.

Tommy noticed Tammi's blackened mood.

"What's wrong, baby?" he asked.

Tammi shook it off and stuck a fork into her organic pancakes, pretending to be hungry. Gladys, and the others, picked up on it, too.

"What could be the matter, Tammi?" Gladys lifted her arms to the sky and turned her face to the sun. She reveled in nature, swaying back and forth, causing her breasts to mimic a grandfather clock. "The day is gorgeous."

Tommy took Tammi's chin in his hand and turned her eyes to his. He knew, he could see the cloudiness there.

"You're safe here, you know that, right?"

Tammi nodded. "Yeah," she managed to squeak out.

"The things that happened all that time ago with those awful women are done. You started over, here." Tommy knew her, deep down, inside and out.

Tammi looked up, tears welling in her eyes.

"Right!" Archie chimed in. He stood, along with Martin and Latoria, and they circled the poor girl.

"You were honest with us in the beginning," Latoria said, "and we'll be honest with you till the end. You are one of us, girl!"

"Exactly," Martin managed to get out before sneaking

back to his pancakes and deftly moving Tammi's plate to his side of the picnic table.

The group hugged, pressing the flesh of their bodies together in a natural, non-sexual way. One couldn't tell where each council member stopped and the other began, except for Latoria. She was black.

Tammi sniffled a bit more and snuggled into Tommy's chest when the others went back to their breakfast.

"What was that ridiculous nickname they gave you, again?" Tommy asked, laughing.

Tammi joined in, her fears allayed, "Raz."

"That's right, wow. And they think we're squares!" Tommy laughed again and hugged Tammi close.

She wasn't completely honest with them. Oh, Tammi didn't lie, but she didn't tell the whole truth, either. It wasn't just Raz. Her full name was Razmatazz. Mama Turk gave her that name the first time Tammi performed on the gang leader. At the time, Mama said there had been nothing like Tammi before and would be nothing like her since. Tammi didn't think much of it, then, but now she realized that Mama was in love.

And love'll make you do crazy shit.

***

What was left of the clerk was in five separate pieces and oozing viscera and various other bodily fluids onto the dust of the parking lot.

Mama Turk chuckled as she lit a Marlboro. She leaned against her bike, the glow from the preceding event still radiating off of her in waves. Her crotch was still warm, not only from the clerk but the events that led up to his unfortunate passing.

Mama got her licks in, that's for sure. Vixen was next, being second in command. Mama's lieutenant rode the poor kid like a rodeo bronco and Mama thought he would give it up right there. He managed to get up one last time and Half-Pint snuck in for the final go round, getting her rocks off as the exhausted young man gave it the college try, but just couldn't stick around when Sideshow took a turn. Too bad, too; he wasn't half bad.

Punishment, according the Scissor Sister by-laws, was swiftly meted out. Centerfold, Sideshow, Diabla and Inga were left out in the cold, so to speak, so they got the honors. Oh, they wouldn't go long without a little satisfaction, Sideshow would see to that, and the four of them would live up to the gang name, but the clerk had failed and, as promised, he wouldn't be allowed to survive.

Each of the four girls removed the ½ inch chains that every Scissor Sister kept in her saddlebag (in case a gang war broke out, or the cops got too cheeky) and affixed one end of the chain to their bikes and the other to one of the clerk's limbs. Nearly dehydrated from spilling so much sweat and bodily fluids for the past hour, he hardly noticed. When those bikes rumbled to life, though, he perked up.

Mama counted down from ten, watching the whole scene dawn on the clerk's face. When she got to one, each of the girls popped their clutches and the bikes jumped forward. With that amount of horsepower on each limb, the poor young man was quartered instantly. His joints tore from the sockets, sounding like a dog tearing into a thick steak. The bikes pulled away, dragging arms and legs. The girls stopped quickly and turned, eager to watch the big finale.

Before shock could set in and before he could bleed out, the clerk picked his head up off of the ground to see what remained of his body. Shoulder and thigh stumps gushed blood with each pump of the young man's heart. The arcs of crimson reached shorter and shorter distances as the clerk bled out into the parking lot, turning the dirty concrete around him into a burgundy mud puddle.

Mama watched the light fade from the clerk's eyes and smiled. She would never get tired of seeing that… ever. She felt her hot button push itself against the tight, leather crotch of her pants but refused to take matters into her own hands. She would wait for that.

"All right, bitches, saddle up!" Mama Turk called out.

Sideshow sat up quickly from between Inga's thighs and took a deep breath. Inga roared in pleasure, bellowing her glee to the slowly fading sunlight. Sideshow smiled and wiped her mouth; Inga was the last Sister to get taken care of.

"Hell yeah!" Sideshow called out.

Inga grunted and pulled her jeans and chaps on. The rest of the girls swung their legs over their hogs and fired up the engines. Mama followed suit and pulled forward, ready to lead the group onto the highway. She waited as Inga and Sideshow caught up, finally turning back and addressing her troops.

"Ladies, we're almost there. Just to make me feel better, what do we do with traitors?"

The gang, as one, called out "Fuck her up!"

"How do we do it?" Mama asked, louder than before.

"Make her bleed!" They called again.

Mama smiled. Raz, and whoever she was shacking up with, wouldn't know what hit them. Mama eyed Vixen and her steely gaze was returned.

Mama turned again and held her fist high. The girls followed suit and waited for Mama to lead the way. Mama's sex still throbbed, aching for any kind of release, but she just gritted her teeth and fought through the pain. Before she let Vixen have Raz, Mama had one more date with that glorious mouth.

"Roll out!" Mama called, dropping her fist and flying forward. The Scissor Sisters, death in their wake, headed out down Route 66.

And these girls were going to get their kicks, whether anyone liked it or not.

***

An impromptu volleyball game came as a Sunday highlight for the residents of Raw Life. The council, on friendly terms, was challenged by a group of residents in a four on four battle. Gladys and Archie took opposite sides of the net to serve as line judges. A small handful of other residents gathered around to watch.

Tommy, being the most athletic, captained the council's team. He positioned his players in a diamond formation with Tammi at the head. She had a killer spike. Latoria readied for battle on Tommy's right and Martin, looking deathly afraid of anything athletic, stood on his left. Tommy called out to the opposing team as he prepared to serve.

"You guys ready?"

The group across the net smiled and cheered. Tommy, breaking into a big grin, raised the volleyball.

"Zero serving zero," he said before tossing the ball in the air. He leapt and served, the slap of his hand on the ball only slightly louder than the smack of Tommy's large scrotum against his own thigh.

The battle raged, back and forth. Breasts flailed, volleyballs volleyed, back and forth, up and over the net. Even with Martin the sides were pretty evenly matched. The sound of genitals slapping against skin in a rough and tumble athletic competition formed a staccato beat akin to a tribal call to arms.

Neither team gave an inch, and the universal twenty-one rule quickly signaled a near conclusion to the game. Back to their initial formation, Tommy again readied to serve. He wiped the sweat from his eye and caught Tammi's glance. She nodded, giving him the encouragement he needed.

"Twenty serving twenty. Game point," Tommy

called out.

The Raw Life Nudist Colony rumbled, as if a minor earthquake had suddenly hit. Before Tommy could even toss the ball for his last, killer serve, the very ground beneath his feet shook.

"Just one of those California quakes," Martin half-joked to the panicked assemblage. He laughed and the others followed suit, nervously.

Tammi knew better, though. She knew what shaking ground was a harbinger of. She had been the cause of it more times than she could count. Tammi turned to Tommy, tears streaming from her eyes.

"I'm sorry," she said.

"What, baby? It's just an earthqua…" Tommy stopped short. The rumbling continued, but now it had a chorus of engines to harmonize with.

In the distance, dust and devilry in their wake, the Scissor Sisters barreled down onto the assembled residents of the Raw Life Nudist Colony. As they approached, Tammi could see the glint and sparkle of sunshine on the large chains that the gang member swung over their heads. Tammi dropped to her knees.

"Run, all of you!" She screamed. "Run for your lives!" Tammi held her head in her hands and just waited for the inevitable.

Latoria, Martin, Gladys and Archie looked at one another. Peace-loving nudists generally didn't have a course of action to repel an invading force. They just stood, staring at the oncoming horde, unable to discern, exactly, what approached. The other residents followed suit.

Tommy knelt next to Tammi and tried to pull her up, but the perspiration from the game caused his hands to slip off. Tammi looked up at her fellow nudists.

"Why aren't they running? WHY AREN'T YOU

RUNNING?"

"Who are those people, Tammi? What do they want?" Tommy asked.

"Me. They want me. It's them."

"*Them*, them?"

"Yes. Why won't anyone run?! Save yourselves!" Tammi beseeched her friends, but they were caught like possum in headlights.

The Sisters were almost upon them. Over the din of the bikes, blood curdling war cries rang out further rooting the nudists to the spot.

Tommy, stood and stepped in front of Tammi. Everyone else may be too hippie to help, but his character, forged in organized sports as a child, wouldn't let him abandon the woman he loved.

"Go, Tommy!" Tammi cried.

"Never, baby," he growled.

And then hell spilled itself all over Raw Life.

Mama Turk led her gaggle of over-sexed hooligans into the colony and circled the group of naked pacifists with their bikes. Around and around they rode, chains swinging over their heads. The only thing the nudists could do was to huddle closer together as the bikes pushed them in closer and closer.

Archie and Gladys managed to meet in the middle of the huddle. They took one another's hands and looked into each other's eyes. They knew the inevitable outcome.

Tammi looked up to them, tears streaming from their eyes. "I'm so sorry…" she said.

Gladys looked down, smiling. She stroked Tammi's cheek. "You should be," Gladys said. "This is all your fault." Gladys turned back to Archie as Tammi hung her head and sobbed.

"Look! We'll give you the bitch, just leave us alone!"

Latoria called out to the bikers, frantic.

Tommy spun on her. "Never!" he bellowed.

Martin stepped forward, joining Latoria. "No, we're pretty sure you can have her!"

The rest of the colonists raised their voices in agreement with Martin.

Tommy stepped in front of Tammi, taking a defensive position.

Mama signaled and the bikes slowed, finally stopping. She slipped off, chain in hand. The rest of the Sisters sat on their bikes as they idled.

"Raz is coming with us," she said to Tommy. "And I don't care how big your dick is, it ain't bigger than my chain, punk."

Archie and Gladys, hand in hand, stepped forward.

"Ms... ummm, Ms...?" Archie stammered.

"Mama," Mama answered.

"Ms. Mama. We don't have any real attachment to this girl, really. We took her in and taught her the nudist lifestyle, but that's as far as it goes. You can take her, and Tommy, for all we care. Just don't hurt us."

Mama nodded, thinking it over. She looked over at Tommy, who was seething.

"Whaddya think of that, tough guy? Looks like the shriveled nuts on this geezer are made of steel."

"He's a backstabbing traitor. Tammi is one of us and you'll have to go through me to get to her!"

Mama sighed and turned back to her girls. "Ladies," she said, "It looks like, uhh, Tammi, has really found a home here... we should let her be in peace."

The nudists smiled and an excited murmur shot through the crowd. Gladys squeezed Archie's hand while Latoria and Martin hugged, being very careful to avoid any genital to genital contact.

Tammi sobbed even harder and stopped just short of wailing.

The Sisters smiled and lowered their chains. Mama spun around, arms wide. "In our world we settle every dispute with a hug, is that all right?"

Archie, excited, stepped forward. "So do we!" He moved into Mama's waiting arms.

Tommy had never let his guard down and knew he was right when Tammi whimpered behind him.

"Don't let him, Tommy…"

Before Tommy could move, Mama and Archie embraced. With a deft twist of the wrist, Mama produced a switchblade and, after the press of a button, had that blade extended and jammed it into Archie's throat. She held him close, digging in with the blade, making the hole in his neck wider and wider.

The nudists stood, staring in shock. Gladys reached out, screaming. Tommy, reflexively, moved closer to Tammi.

Mama threw the knife to the ground and plunged her hand into the large hole she had just created in Archie's neck. The blood poured from the wound and Archie convulsed causing his flaccid penis to dance like a marionette. Mama rooted around in the wound for a moment until she found what she was looking for. From inside Archie's throat, she pulled out his tongue and draped it onto his chest.

"Look, I dressed him up!" Mama called to her girls, who roared with laughter. "He's got a Brazilian necktie now!"

Mama laughed herself and threw Archie to the ground. She sauntered to her bike and hopped on. She looked over at the group of nudists, huddling together.

"You freaks are a piece of work. Pacifists? Living off the land? Jesus Christ, I'd pay half of you to put your clothes back on!" Mama and the Sisters exploded into laughter once again.

Gladys shook herself free of the fear and dropped to her knees. She took Archie's head into her lap, resting it on her voluminous gray pubic hair like a pillow as the light left his eyes.

"Ladies, eat these freaks up!" Mama cried and the Sisters sprang into action.

Tommy was the first to take a glancing blow from a glittering, swinging chain. He crumpled to the ground, unconscious. No matter how much Tammi shook him or beseeched her hero to get up, he simply would not move.

The Sisters waded into the nudists, chains spinning. Metal gleamed in the sunlight and ripped skin from bone. The Raw Lifers tried to escape, but Mama's girls were very good at what they did. Chains stripped flesh from breasts and backs, scrotums and labia alike. Blood flowed like a river as each of the nudists fell before the vile gang.

Sideshow, tongue flailing, relished beating Martin down with her chain. Blow after blow rained onto the dumpy accountant and, long after his squealing had ceased, she continued the assault. Martin's spinal column was reduced to a mushy gruel, finally causing Sideshow to turn her attention elsewhere.

Half-Pint wended her way in and out of her naked victims, slicing a hamstring here and an Achilles' tendon there. The nudists fell to the ground, howling in pain. Behind Half-Pint, Diabla followed her shorter Sister using the long heels of her boots to stomp holes in the eye sockets, bellies, necks… any soft spot she could find. Diabla had a special penchant for slamming that high-heeled dagger into any errant testicles she could find, smashing them like grapes in an effort to make a deviant version of a rocky mountain wine. The jellied remnants of many a manhood littered the volleyball court.

Through the carnage, Gladys rocked back and forth with

Archie's rapidly cooling head in her lap. Vixen sauntered up to the old lady, chain swinging.

"Ain't you afraid of me, old bitch?" Vixen asked, showing proper deference to her elder.

Gladys looked up and smiled. "You took away the only reason I had to live, so I don't…"

Vixen's chain smashed into Gladys' head, dislocating the old woman's jaw and removing an eye as it smacked her to the side. Unconscious when she hit the ground, Gladys' disfigured face bled out through multiple wounds.

Vixen chuckled as she stepped over the dying nudist and shook her head. "You talk too much, hippie."

Inga swaggered up to Latoria and cracked her oversized knuckles. The sound and force of the large bones smacking against one another thudded into Latoria who, instinctively, shivered.

Tiny, compared to the hulking Nordic behemoth, Latoria scrunched her eyes shut and covered her head, as she had been taught to do in school when faced with a natural disaster. When no blow came after a moment, Latoria peeked out from between her fingers to find that Inga had removed her pants and stood in front of the nudist, naked from the waist down.

Used to nudity as a way of life, Latoria was still unprepared for what stood before her. If she didn't know better, she would have assume she was staring at the genitals of a teenage boy with a small penis but… this was a grown, an overgrown, woman. *Post-op tranny*, Latoria thought but quickly dismissed that. *Why would the penis be so small?* And then it hit her. Latoria wasn't looking at an undersized penis, but an oversized clitoris. Red and throbbing, the sexual nerve center of this leviathan of a woman pointed at Latoria, as if indicating what *it* wanted. Latoria resumed her disaster prevention pose.

"You make Inga feel yummy, you get to live," the enormous Scissor Sister said.

Latoria looked up. Before she could answer, Inga grabbed her by the head like a basketball and shoved the poor woman's head into her crotch and onto the warm, pulsating center of her desire.

Latoria struggled mightily, mouth open and tongue flapping against Inga's clitoris. Oxygen came in small bursts, but not enough for Latoria to ever catch her breath. She felt herself going in and out of consciousness. To make matters worse, in her ecstasy, Inga was not paying attention to the amount of pressure that she applied to Latoria's skull. Starved of oxygen as her skull slowly pressed in against her brain, Latoria was, effectively, drowning in Inga's musk.

Inga, if she knew what was happening, gave no indication that it mattered. The big girl writhed and shook, never letting Latoria escape. Even as the poor girl quaked, going into seizure-like death throes as she suffocated pressed into Inga's labia, the biker gave no quarter.

Inga came, hard, with waves of pleasure rocking through her body as Latoria died from a combination of the lack of oxygen and two, parallel skull fractures. Inga dropped the corpse to the ground.

"Ladies, mount up!" Mama called out.

Inga pulled her tight jeans and chaps back on, for the second time that day, and did as she was told.

Mama surveyed the nudist colony and smiled at the carnage. Naked hippies littered the area. Only Raz was unscathed… physically. Mama took off her Scissor Sisters jacket and walked up to the weeping Raz. She draped the jacket around her shoulders and pulled the girl up to a standing position.

"You ready to go, Raz?" Mama asked.

Razmatazz sobbed heavily, but managed to nod. It was

inevitable. She would never be free of them.

At their feet, Tommy groaned. He reached up at them, fighting through the fog and the pain. He would never let Tammi go. Never.

Mama raised her boot, ready to smash Tommy's skull in and end this shit once and for all.

"Mama?" Raz managed to squeak out, wiping her eyes with the sleeves of the jacket.

Mama turned. She missed hearing that. She missed her best girl. "Yeah, baby?"

"Please, don't hurt Tommy anymore. He was good to me."

Mama looked down at the nude athlete with nothing but spite, but lowered her boot. She could never tell Razmatazz no.

"Okay, baby doll, this one gets a pass." Mama turned to the rest of the girls. "You heard me, mount up! We got miles to go before we sleep… and you bitches know what I mean by sleep. HA!"

Mama, tugging Raz behind her, got the bike and swung her leg over. Raz, muscle memory taking over, followed suit.

"We'll get you some pants on the way, girl," Mama said.

Raz sniffled and nodded. She turned back to watch Tommy. He just stared at her. Broken. She blew him a kiss and then turned, grabbing Mama around the waist as the bike spit gravel and sped off toward the horizon.

The Sisters followed. The roar of the bikes shaking the Earth was the last thing Tommy remembered before blacking out.

Except for a few things. He vowed to get Tammi back. He vowed to avenge the deaths of his friends. And, right before everything faded, he swore he would one day reach his hand into Mama Turk's chest and rip out her black heart. He would then spike it like a football.

CRYPTIDS!

MISTY HILLS OF DREAMER SHEEP

Called back for my uncle's funeral, I had never planned on stepping foot within the confines of Chimney Rock, North Carolina again. The foothills of the Appalachian Mountains met the Piedmont Plateau and Chimney Rock stood as ageless as the mountains it introduced. It was a typical rural area where a sickly lad with a penchant for reading stories of a fantastic nature was not be exalted for his literary aspirations and quick wit.

I had never known my father and my mother died during childbirth. The locals, of course, believed I was cursed. My uncle, under some kind of duress, agreed to raise me. A cattle farmer by trade, he regarded me as nothing more than another piece of livestock. Scarlet fever and a heart condition plagued my early years and, if it had been legal, Uncle Vernon would have liked nothing more than to "put me down" like a diseased foal.

Blessedly, Chimney Rock had a small library. Two rooms were apportioned by the town fathers to provide a library for the use of the community. These rooms were only utilized as a library in order for Chimney Rock to meet the qualifications to receive farm community Federal aid since it was cheaper than building a health clinic.

Being the only library customer in town, I had the distinct pleasure of perusing the works of Lovecraft and Poe, of Matheson and Derleth and Keeler and Asimov. The paperbacks were the only books affordable enough for our library and they opened my eyes to new worlds.

Uncle Vernon would not allow those types of books and magazines in his home. For all his brusqueness, he was a cowardly man who saw the Devil in anything that he didn't understand. This included me. He never physically laid a hand on me but there were moments of loneliness where I would have welcomed any hand... even one raised in violence. Alone, I found myself venturing into the foothills of Appalachia which, despite everything, felt like home. It sprawled open and wide and, at the same time, was choked with vegetation and was as claustrophobic as a tomb. It was me and I it. Aspiration versus reality.

In my frequent visits to the wooded areas, I would run across half-inebriated hunters attempting to stay camouflaged in their cheap tree blinds. Careful to remain out of sight (and with the level of moonshine involved with a majority of these men it was fairly easy). One day, I overheard two hunters talking about a creature of enormous size and strength that lived in these very hills.

At first, I assumed that the men were speaking of a Sasquatch, that mythical Bigfoot. I was wrong, though, for these men were speaking of a creature that only appeared in the Appalachian Mountains and was as vile, vicious and dangerous as any other creature imaginable. They were speaking of the sheepsquatch.

I started, unprepared for that particular word. Of course, in this backward town the local myth would be something as utterly ridiculous as a sheepsquatch! Invariably, like all of these stories, an uncle of a friend's cousin had encountered the vile and savage sheepsquatch while hunting. The man put up a brave countenance, but could not fight the fear. The thing stood eight feet tall and was covered in wooly white and gray fleece. It was bipedal and massively wide. It had arms and hands and opposable thumbs. It looked extremely powerful, to the terrified hunter. Most horrendous of all, was the head of the sheepsquatch. Unlike sheep, the creature possessed a mouth of razor-like teeth, set in a snouted face. The sheepsquatch had yellow, watery eyes and a pair of curved horns that ended in stiletto points. According to the hunters, the sheepsquatch roared, bared its sharp teeth, and lunged at the terrified witness who turned and ran into the night.

Barely suppressing a giggle, I moved through the underbrush away from the duo in the tree blind but eager to learn more.

I arrived at the library earlier than usual to research more about this silly creature only to find that the librarian had died and with him so went the library. I finished out my schooling in Chimney Rock and left for university with an academic scholarship and student loans, vowing to never return.

Uncle Vernon died ten years later. His wife, Irene, passed earlier and the couple was childless. This made me the only living heir (much to my uncle's chagrin, I assume) and required me to return to Chimney Rock in order to sell the property. That and be done with it once and for all.

Money was a necessity. I had studied literature in school and fancied myself an author. I had published two short stories and was currently shopping a novel of the macabre. It wasn't going well. To supplement my income, I taught English to foreign nationals visiting Washington, D.C.

I needed Vernon's money.

Entering town I passed the abandoned library and that triggered a change in plans. I turned away from my uncle's home and drove to those footlands. Even as bitter as I was, I had to admit that I missed the mists at dusk. The beautiful solitude beckoned.

Crunching through foliage, I thought of the starry nights and muggy days that I followed these exact same paths. I stopped and looked up at the treetops as the sun faded from view and realized this was the area where I heard the sheep-squatch story. I laughed out loud and, quite unlike me, I called out into the night.

"Sheepsquatch! I'm here so, by all means, make yourself known to me so we can put an end to this!"

I laughed again. I was a blithering fool but, on my salary, this was the only therapy I could afford. I waited, more to savor the moment in the region than anything else.

A deep, powerful voice floated from the dense forest. "Howard Fence, I have come to speak with you."

I stopped short. The bullies of my youth had pulled pranks and made jokes at my expense for years. Seeing the obituary would mean their favorite target had returned. No longer a frail boy, I spun, ready for vengeance. What greeted me was no practical joke.

Standing before me was the sheepsquatch exactly like the hunters had described. I screamed and fell backwards, falling on my rear end, and attempted to scoot away. The sheep-squatch raised a hand and bade me to stop. Far less angry than I had heard him described, he was even polite.

"Please. Howard Fence, I have need of you."

This stopped me. The sheepsquatch, legendary creature of the Appalachians, had need of me. As if to placate me even more, the sheepsquatch squatted on his powerful legs and made it down into a sitting position, facing me.

"Uh… uh… uh…" I managed to say.

The sheepsquatch smiled. He laughed and shook his head. The laugh was friendly but hoarse, as if he had infrequent occasion to use his voice.

"You must tell my tale," he said.

"Me?"

The sheepsquatch stood and approached. He laid an enormous hand on my head. It had an intense heat, but did not burn. At the moment of his touch, the sheepsquatch 'spoke' to me. The best description I have of this moment is that he *emptied*. His thoughts, his dreams and, most importantly, his story, filled me to the point of bursting. I agreed, with a thought. The choice was obvious and no storyteller, even a self-professed one, could turn down an offer of this magnitude. It was now my task to tell the tale of the sheepsquatch; I had become the bard of an elder god!

The sheepsquatch was relieved that I had returned. He had known of me, of course, and waited until I would traipse through the land of my birth one more time. He was bound to this region, more out of familiarity and need (but that is part of his tale) and he rarely encountered humans. Furthermore, of those humans he encountered, none of them were adequately prepared to be a recorder of deeds. Chimney Rock, as one can surmise, wasn't a hotbed of intellectual curiosity. Of all the humans that the sheepsquatch had encountered in the woods, none possessed enough cognitive faculties to act as bard for this powerful, majestic creature. Desperate for a human to carry on his tale, the sheepsquatch angrily menaced any he found unable to fulfill the needs of his legacy. The myth persisted and the locals spread the story of a violent beast.

He was no beast. He was noble.

His story was unlike any other.

55 B.C. Roman Centurions invaded Northern Britannia, raping and pillaging without regard. Rome had picked the perfect time to invade. Just before winter, all able-bodied warriors were on extended hunts intended to provide sustenance to last through the oncoming harsh winter. The Roman army went from village to village, forcing their laws, their faith, and their 'civilization' on the early Celts.

In battle, the Celts were far superior. The Celts, large and sinewy, fought in furs with axes. They were fierce. Unfortunately, one warrior, no matter how skilled, could not defeat a legion of Caesar's men, no matter how unskilled.

Caesar himself was awed by the Celtic warriors. He studied them, and the Druid Priests, hoping to learn the source of their unyielding spirit. He went as far as to capture a younger Druid and had him tortured. The man was beaten, bled, and pinched with hot pincers trying to get to the secret of the Celt's fighting prowess.

A conquering army would many times assimilate some of the conquered people's religion, making the transition easier. Through Caesar's "persuasion" he learned much more than the customs of the Druidic Celts. He learned their secrets, their ancient arcane rights and he learned the key to their avatar, the source of their ferocity!

Julius Caesar, new Lord of Britannia, learned the secret of calling the Gafr, the Goat, the Celtic demi-god Gabrus and would bring him to Rome. The tortured Druid gave Caesar the secret of conjuring and controlling the Gafr. The nefarious Caesar intended to do just that.

In Rome, Caesar performed the ritual. The incantation took three components. One of animal: the severed head of a large goat and one of man: the massive body of a headless gladiator. Caesar wore a pendant around his neck with Celtic symbols created under the exact specifications of the half-dead Druid he had fed to the dogs in Britannia. It glowed. This was the third component: one of magic. It would bind the souls of man and beast together and, hopefully, become more than the sum of its parts.

The head of the goat knit itself to the body of the gladiator, during the incantations. Head grafted to body and the two became one, infused with the power of an ancient land. Upon its completion, its self-surgery, the Celtic God of Justice and War lived again under the command of Julius Caesar. In that moment, Rome overtook the Celtic culture completely.

The Gafr, the Goat God, elder and eternal, stood before Julius Caesar. Bound by the pendant to obey, the Gafr stood ready to serve. Caesar admired his beast (for that is what he thought he had in his possession) never realizing that the power at his command was only limited by the boundaries of Earth, on which the Gafr rarely stepped.

The Empire would have trembled if not for the pettiness of Caesar. His only use for the Gafr was as a conversation piece. In order to scare the Senate, the Gafr accompanied Caesar throughout the land. Not all of Rome was taken with Caesar's new "pet," as the Gafr was called. Two nobles in particular, Brutus and Cassius, held a distinct disdain for the pagan monstrosity before them.

As the sheepsquatch travelled with Caesar he would often times come in contact with Brutus and Cassius. The Gafr, of course, was well aware of the nobles' plans. Although a servant of Caesar, he was an unwilling one. The ritual forced the Gafr to obey Julius, but not to protect him. When asked what, if anything, the Caesar could fear with the sheepsquatch behind him, the Gafr responded, "Beware the Ides of March." Caesar laughed at his companions joke carried on, never heeding the words of a god. The Gafr knew Caesar would pay no mind and smiled at the thought of freedom.

Caesar believed himself to be invincible. Unconcerned with the threat of assassination, Caesar ordered the Gafr to remain at the palace as he went to the Senate. There, Brutus plunged a knife into his leader's back. The date was March 14th.

Brutus ripped the pendant from around Caesar's neck and hid it away, afraid of what uses it may have.

The master died, the servant was liberated and, for many years, the Gafr lived in peace on the outskirts of the city. Until a young heir-apparent to the throne of Rome discovered the secret of Julius Caesar. The pendant that controlled the demi-god was found. An involuntary shudder ran through all the citizens of Rome as the pendant holding the Gafr's soul was discovered by a sixteen-year-old Nero on the eve before his ascension.

54 A.D. Nero took the throne of Rome from the murdered Emperor Claudius. After over 100 years of peaceful existence, the Gafr was called into service once again. Following Julius' instructions, the young Nero called the Gafr to his side.

As distasteful as service to Julius was, service to Nero was abhorrent. Where Caesar used the Gafr to gain public interest and wrest power from a terrified Senate, Nero found the Gafr an amusing tool of destruction. Nothing stood in Nero's way... no man, woman, or child. The sheepsquatch was ordered to murder with callous disregard; Nero's madness knew no boundaries.

A Celtic god of justice, reduced by "civilization" to a murderous thug, The Gafr wept and longed for Nero's death. Caesar served as an amusing diversion but this Nero was evil incarnate.

The Emperor commanded the Gafr to do the unimaginable. The power of the pendant holding the Gafr's soul was so strong that under Nero's command, the Gafr burned Rome to the ground.

Nero delighted in the carnage. The Gafr had done his

bidding! He watched the city burn, its people burn... all from the safety of his own balcony. How dare the people tell him what we will build or will not build... he was the Emperor of Rome!

As Nero would often say, to anyone within earshot, "Rome wishes? I am Rome!"

Unfortunately for Nero, the Gafr was in earshot many of those times and returned to the balcony after setting the city ablaze.

The sheepsquatch scooped Nero up and held him high over his head. Nero should have been more careful how he phrased his last command to the Gafr.

"Burn Rome to the ground! All of Rome!" Nero had said.

Nero's fall was thought to be a suicide. Remorse for his burning of Rome, historian's thought. By all accounts, Nero was remorseful in his last moments, so remorseful he wished he never had enslaved the Gafr.

Amidst the blood and gore on the street, the pendant controlling the Gafr sat. The Gafr had hoped to gain possession of it, hide it... forever. Before he could retrieve the accursed thing, refugees from the city filled the street. They rushed toward and over the corpse of Nero. Women holding children, men carrying baskets... everyone fled Rome and, with them, the pendant disappeared.

The Gafr could feel the pendant calling to him, but was never able to find exactly where it had been hidden. He followed the siren's call of the damned thing for millennia, eventually coming to the new world. The Appalachian Mountains called to him, reminding the sheepsquatch of his ancient Britannic home.

He 'heard' the pendant. It was here, in America, and it was relatively close. He could no longer walk the Earth unencumbered, though. He was desperate to find the pendant, but had to remain hidden, finding solitude and contentment in the forest.

I accepted his call and, as one can tell, intend to deliver the tale of the sheepsquatch to the world as well as find the pendant. I believe I will not be selling my uncle's farm after all and, upon returning to Washington, D.C., a visit to The Smithsonian may be in order.

In the meantime, he will wait, like always, perpetuating the myth of rabid beast to whatever unlucky souls manage to cross the sheepsquatch's path. After all, what is 2000 years to an immortal?

ZOMBIES!

END SCENE

"Jesus H. Christ, cut!"

The whirring of the Panavision camera slowly tapered off as Robert Crone, hack filmmaker and exploitive genius, stalked from behind the camera and onto the set. The crew shrunk back into the shadows as far as they could to avoid the oncoming tirade. Crone had been in a foul mood for approximately the last forty years, but things had become more and more desperate in the last few. 1968 was proving to be another clunker of a release schedule and there was only so much money the studio could afford to lose and that meant the Crone was on the chopping block.

And when Crone was on the chopping block, everyone was on the chopping block. Especially the actors or, as Crone lovingly referred to them, 'the talking meat.' All of this culminated in the great director's current fury on the set of *Vampire Lust Goddess*, an average Crone film derivative of the genre fare that had made him quite a bit of money in the early 1960s.

He pushed his way through the ring of druidic cult extras and onto the sacrificial alar set (the same one used for

Cannibal Sacrifice, times were certainly tough) and stood eye to nipple with Faye Worthington, ingénue du jour (real name Penelope Flossom) and current Crone Girl. She was suspended by her arms above the altar and corn syrup blood dripped down her fine, naked body and pooled in her pubic hair. The casting process insured that Crone was quite familiar with that entire region and this was business.

"Awww, c'mon Bobby! What'd I do wrong?" Faye whined, the awkward plastic vampire teeth muffling her a bit.

"Wrong? Nothing, baby. You didn't do anything wrong… you are just horrible!" Crone shot back.

That hung there, thick as fog. The druidic extras shuffled nervously and none of the crew emerged from the relative safety of the darkened studio outside the lit set.

The silence was broken by a single sniffle from Ms. Worthington. This escalated quickly and, in under ten seconds, she was in the middle of a full-blown episode complete with tears, caterwauling and histrionics.

Crone threw up his hands and headed off set toward the office. "Cut her down. Take fifteen. Fuck that, break for lunch."

No one mentioned that is was only nine in the morning as the crew swooped in, lowering Ms. Worthington (soon to go back to Flossom, one would suppose) to the ground noting that Crone must be getting soft. In the flush years he would have let her swing through lunch.

Crone entered the small office and slammed the door behind himself. He was in the seat and a bottle of Old Granddad whiskey were to his lips in record time.

"Jesus H. Christ," he said to himself. Not out of any kind of belief, but because it just sounded appropriate.

Crone glanced up at the walls of the office. Lurid, exploitation film posters marked the walls. Each of them more successful than the last. *Vampegeddon*, *Blood Orgy of the Damned*, *Desert Man-Beast* and so many more reflected Crone's successes over the previous decade, but things were different now. Just a few years ago, the average mouth-breathing American could turn on the nightly news and see a war. A real, life or death, war playing out on their TV screen and Crone had struggled to keep pace. The kids that went in droves to see *Werewolf Gym Teacher* in droves at the drive-in in 1959 are not the teenagers of today.

Crone knocked back another shot and went immediately to the gallows humor. Most of those kids are dying on that TV screen right now, he thought. How could he compete with that? Naked vampires? Bright red corn syrup and panty-hose filled with cotton? Blood and guts were the new American dinner conversation.

A knock on the door went ignored at first. Another shot. Another knock. Crone sighed.

"Go the fuck away!"

"Sir! This is important."

Muffled by the door, his assistant's voice sounded urgent. Marlene knew not to interrupt him so what kind of bullshit is this.

Sighing again, Crone stood and opened the door. Standing before him was Marlene. Usually mousy and bright, her big glasses magnifying her eyes to epic proportions, she was no looker (according to Crone) she just stood there, tears streaming down her cheeks. She held a transistor radio up.

"What the hell is this, Marlene…"

"Just listen," she hissed. Crone was taken aback, Marlene was never this direct. When he did take a minute to hear the news broadcast from the radio, the whole world changed for Crone. All at once.

"… again. We must report the unbelievable. It seems, no it is true, it is real, that dead people. People formerly dead have come back to life and are eating the living. This level of mass psychosis or… dear God, I don't know what to call this. The station doesn't want me to tell you this, but… it is the end of times, listeners. The dead walk. The Lord Himself will soon walk the Earth and we…"

Crone slowly wrapped his hand around Marlene's and shut the radio off. Without a word he turned toward the posters and toasted them with the bottle of Old Granddad. Robert Crone didn't really believe he had just listened to the preamble of the End of the World, but he was pretty sure this would be the end of his world. A war was bad enough, how could he compete with living dead cannibals?

Another shot and *Vampire Lust Goddess* stopped production. The world itself went to hell but there as a reason people called Robert Crone the Hollywood Cockroach. He would not go quietly into that night. He would not say die. He was not through exploiting anything he could his hands on.

Six months into the worldwide crisis and Robert Crone finally figured out what he needed to do. He would simply give the people a spectacle. Something they couldn't see out their windows or on their TV screens.

He would give them real cinema.

The idea came innocently enough. Los Angeles was a nexus for this zombie, or whatever you call it, outbreak. The concentration of people, filth, and an absolute disregard for one another was the perfect formula for the contagion to be very virulent. It wasn't uncommon to see violent clashes between a shambling wreck of a human being and something that used to be dead at any given point in one's day. Sometimes you couldn't tell the combatants apart without a program. Crone was careful, though, and protected himself as he went to and from the studio, trying desperately to get things going again. He noticed that these creatures didn't really feel pain. They were oblivious, like hippies, and only went down with a bit of head trauma. The idea gestated as he tried, in vain, to recoup the losses from shutting down *Vampire Lust Goddess* and then, like a little bit of head trauma of his own, it hit him.

Don't work against the system... work with it. Crone couldn't believe he had forgotten the golden rule that started him in the business. *Don't swim upstream, you asshole*, he berated himself after coming to THE conclusion.

The film industry was impacted by the global crisis, of course, but you can't kill that beast either. No matter the tragedy and no matter the continent spanning horrors the world faced everyone still had a couple of bucks to forget about life for a while. The problem, like before, was not being able to trump real life. Crone spent all of his time after the outbreak trying to get to that epiphany that would change his fortunes.

It finally came in the guise of Penelope Flossom, of all people.

Crone pulled into the lot of the small offices he rented after being forced from the studio. He deftly dodged a couple of the dead headers but his mouth dropped as another one of them shambled from the darkness of the alley next to the office building. He knew what he should do. The living all across the country adapted to the presence of the living dead fairly well. It was an odd arrangement but it worked. School curriculums added advanced physiology and outdoor survival classes and each of them stressed using the 'head shot' to take out the enemy. The enemy, of, course, were the dead and the good guys were alive. So, men women and children had taken to the streets disposing of as many dead as they could find. This is what Crone was working toward and he trained diligently. He turned the car and pointed the headlight directly at the dead head coming out of the alley.

He stated at the blood-ridden and realized it was Penelope Flossom. Fucking Penelope Flossom, Vampire Lust Queen and shitty actress. Crone's foot strayed from the gas to the brake. He stared at the thing that was Penelope. Barely recognizable, the tell-tale sign for Crone were the dead head's tits. Unmarred, even though they were that strange gray color, the dead head still possessed a magnificent rack. That's the rack that got her the part in *Vampire Lust Queen*... literally. Any number of young, up and coming actresses have straddled Robert Crone to advance their careers, but very few had done so with perfect breasts. He sighed. Even though he didn't give a shit, really, about anyone on the planet HE still had to live there and another dead head out of the picture just made things safer, perfect tits or not.

He gunned the engine and the big Mercury leapt forward and smack dab into Penelope Flossom. The impact was brutal. Probably due to the decomposition, her body flew apart in an odd manner. Her torso, complete with tits (giving Crone a last look) slid across the windshield as if it were surfing on grape jelly. Arms and legs separated at the shoulders and hips respectively, and her head, teeth still gnashing, flew through the air and landed behind the car. Crone heard it crack open like a pumpkin and watched it explode in his rear-view mirror. He smiled, despite the fact it was Penelope, and thought, "Shit. If we could only pull that off on screen. What a freaking picture!"

The epiphany. Right then. Right there. Akin to discovering the power of juxtaposition in the Kuleshov Effect or Edison's brain child and first film studio, The Black Maria, Crone had just changed the film industry for good. It had to be him, though. He needed to keep this a secret and get something shot... fast.

Crone knew how the infernal business worked. Labor wasn't his issue, there were hundreds of actors waiting for that 'big break' where they could get the right exposure and picked up on a big studio film. Shake a palm tree and they would fall out in droves. So he had his cast. Crone was wise enough to keep the Panavision close at hand and hidden from creditors. Camera, check. Crew? Hell, you couldn't go ten feet in this town without running into competent film professionals and all he had to do was avoid the union. Check.

The hard part was getting his new stunt team.

Marlene had stuck it out with him through the 'plague,' the blackballing... all of it. She even stuck it out through that unfortunate paternity case from a few years back concerning the potential Robert Crone, Junior and the lead actress from his biggest moneymaker, *Blood of the Cannibal God*. There was another pair of tits that could sink ships and Marlene was there through it all.

Crone knew she was in love with him. Or, at least, the idea of him. Film producer. Dream maker. She was a bit mousy and flat for his tastes and there was never a big enough storm for him to sail into that port, but she held that torch high and worked her ass off in the meantime. He knew if he got together with Marlene her work would suffer and he didn't know how to do anything but make movies. She managed everything else.

And she was great bait. It only took Crone a minute or two to convince Marlene that she was the only way his new plan would work, which wasn't a lie, and the found themselves on Sunset. This particular section of the city was a hotbed for dead head activity and Crone knew that putting a perfectly edible, and helpless, young woman in the middle of the street would attract dead heads like flies.

It was dangerous, yes, but he felt quite comfortable

behind the wheel of his Mercury. The headlights played across Marlene's shivering body as she stood in the street, scanning furtively back and forth. The police rarely came this way anymore and the dead heads had, really, taken root. There wasn't even any power on this side of the city.

It didn't take long for the first of them to peel out from the shadows. Walking on broken legs and stumps and hands and whatever made them mobile, a pack of dead heads slowly approached the girl.

"Mr. Crone!" Marlene screamed out.

Crone flashed the headlights communicating to Marlene to stay in place and stay with the plan.

The dead heads stepped closer. Robert was nearly close enough to hear the moans. Moaning and the stench of death. Crone wasn't sure how long he could put up with it and mentally made a note to get Marlene some flowers.

Crone waited until the last possible second. Just as the dead heads were ready to bury their faces into Marlene, Crone laid on the horn. Deep and powerful, the blast of sound startled Marlene and, better yet, got the attention of the shambling hoard of the dead.

The herd turned, distracted, and Marlene bolted from them and toward the Mercury. As she slipped into the car breathing heavily, Crone leaned on the horn one more time.

From behind the Mercury a group of production assistants from Cal Berkley working on degrees in film and in need of screen credit burst out from behind the Mercury. With phone books strapped to their bodies, the howling students moved in unison carrying a wind of chicken wire and flanked the group of dead heads.

Like they had practiced, the students deftly avoided the teeth and nails of the dead (or it deflected off of the phone books). Crone squealed in glee as the production assistants wrapped up five of the dead heads and dragged them back toward the Grand Marquis.

From the safety of the Mercury, Crone popped the trunk and one of the largest American cars ever made was soon filled to the brim with five emaciated, shambling corpses. Once the trunk was closed, the production assistants dispersed back into the shadows, per instructions, to rendezvous at the studio.

Crone sat back in the seat and smiled contentedly. Marlene, still shaking, turned to Crone.

"That was the scariest thing I have ever done!"

Crone nodded. He looked up and smiled, taking Marlene's cheek in his hand. She pushed into his touch, honored.

"And you were great," he said. "Just a few more trips and we'll have the whole cast."

Tears welled in Marlene's eyes. "A few more trips?"

CRONE PACED BACK AND FORTH. THE LIGHTS WERE SET up in the studio. Big, bright HMI's that made the dingy joint look like an All-American living room complete with great big TV and complementing tables for watching and eating dinner at the same time. It reeked of normalcy and Crone managed a smile.

Marlene approached, breathless. She looked up at Crone and nodded.

He took a deep breath and cupped his hands around his mouth.

"OK, people! We are only going to have one take at this! Once we get the cast in place we need to rock and roll, you got me?!"

A chorus of 'yesses' and 'yups' echoed in the chamber. Crone turned to his cinematographer.

"Roll camera."

"Speed."

Crone turned to the left and barked into the shadows. "Roll sound!"

"Sound speed."

Crone took another deep breath and called out toward the set. "Bring 'em in!"

From the back of the studio three dead heads shambled forward. They were dressed in average American wardrobe: middle class father, mother, and daughter. The make-up crew had done a spectacular job working on the corpses. Relatively fresh, the dead heads looked alive and kicking.

Three grips, each holding a pole with a looped rope end, commonly used for maneuvering dangerous animals, guided the dead heads to the large, paisley couch and sat them down. The dead heads struggled, but the burly film grips, used to a life of hauling cable and lights, managed to get them in place. Mother, Father and Daughter in front of the television set.

The dead heads gnashed their teeth and lurched forward, trying to get to the fresh meat beyond the lights, but the poles held fast.

Tentatively, Marlene stepped in front of them, just out of reach of the grasping arms. She held the clapper, the slate, in front of the camera. It read: Title - *All-American Horror* / Director – Robert Crone / Camera – Richard Angst. She shook and jumped every time one of the dead heads swiped at her.

"Hold that steady, Marlene!" Crone called from behind the camera.

Marlene nodded and held it up. She opened the clapper. "All-American scene twenty-two, take one." She slapped the slate together with a loud CLACK (so the sound could synch up with the picture) and scooted into the relative safety of the above the liners behind the camera.

"All right. Home invader, take your position!" Crone called out.

The Home Invader, the villain of the masterpiece, took a position next to camera right and danced from foot to foot. Even wearing a ski mask, everyone on set could see just how nervous he was. He danced from foot to foot, eager to get the scene shot and done with. The machete he carried, real metal for this shot, gleamed in the light from the set.

"Let 'em loose and ACTION!" Crone barked.

In a flash the roped poles were loosened from the necks of the dead heads. Being deceased severely affects one's motor skills and the Home Invader leapt into the scene from off camera and brandished the machete before the family could even lurch off the couch.

Like they had rehearsed (with cantaloupe), the Home Invader hacked into the head of each of the family members. Father, then Mother, then Daughter all fell to his blade. He made sure to get each of them right between the uprights first and quell any danger that the dead heads posed to the rest of the cast and crew. After that, every hack, slash and chop was purely an aesthetic choice.

Crone sat behind the camera, mesmerized. Before him one of the vilest and disgusting scenes in cinema history played out. It was visceral. The Home Invader, character actor and good friend Dick Milligan, swung the blade from side to side, high and low. The Father's jaw separated in a wash of gore and black ichor. The Mother saw both arms removed like some decaying Venus. The Daughter caught most of Milligan's attack, being the closest to him, since he nearly cleaved her right in two with the initial strike. This was a cathartic moment for Milligan since he had lost most of his family in the initial wave of dead heads. He jumped at the role.

Stage blood ran like rivers from the crevices in the family's heads. The make-up department noticed early on that the natural blood had coagulated and, therefore, the things were pretty dry inside. Crone thought long and hard. He wanted to give the audience reality… the most real reality they had ever seen but if he kept it too real they would think it was some fake-o attempt at horror. He made the command decision to fill the dead heads brain pans up with stage blood, nearly a gallon each, and boy was he happy he did. The set soon looked like some kind of strange modern art done only in reds and blacks.

Milligan was still hacking away and sobbing into the ski mask when Crone ended the scene.

"Cut!" Robert yelled. The whir of the Panavision stopped and the cinematographer sat back in his chair. Nearly everyone stood down, except for Milligan. He continued to hack his way into the dead head family, yelping as he did so and crying out the name of his own daughter who had perished that first day.

Crone considered yelling cut again but didn't. He'd let the crew take fifteen and Don could take out the rest of his anger on the blood-soaked couch and whatever pieces of the dead heads were left.

"Take fifteen!" Crone yelled and gave the thumbs up to Marlene indicating that she could go, too. He sat and watched Don Milligan get himself right. The man chopped and chopped, sobbing and sniffling, the snot running over the knit fabric of the ski mask, until he couldn't move his arms. Milligan dropped to his knees, splashing in the pool of grue he had just created, and dropped the machete. He sobbed, his body heaving with the enormity of it all. Finally, he raised his head toward the burning lights of the studio and wailed... and then collapsed. Every ounce of strength had left his body and he was spent.

Crone stood and walked over to Milligan, helping him up and pulling the ski mask off.

"Robert," Don managed, "they dead yet?"

Crone smiled and nodded. "Yeah, buddy, they're dead. Go have a smoke and we'll do it again in a bit."

Milligan managed a crooked smile. "Thank you, buddy."

Crone slapped his pal on the back and pushed him toward the door. "My pleasure," he answered and smiled. Milligan was so amped up to get some payback he was doing this below scale. Not only was Crone saving money and doing things that had never been legally committed to film before, he didn't have to deal with any unions or prima donnas. And, at the same time, he was helping the community by getting rid of the dead heads. Win fucking win. It took everything Crone had not to cry out in joy. 'Keep it cool, cat,' he said to himself, 'and get everything ready for the next shot.'

With a spring in his step for the first time in months, Crone snatched the shooting script off of the floor and paged through. This was going to be a long shoot and he squealed with glee as the maintenance crew swooped onto the set to get the area ready for the next scene.

The next sixteen hours flew by in a blur of gore and grue. Crone took the opportunity to commit to film every atrocious act he could think of and, best of all, it was absolutely budget neutral. Marlene only threw up a few times and the crew seemed to genuinely enjoy themselves. There was, virtually, a never-ending supply of 'stunt players' as the living cast and crew had taken to calling the dead heads.

Robert watched in absolute joy as he bashed in heads, sawed off limbs... any manner of debauched death was possible. He actually had a child drawn and quartered. The little boy couldn't have been more than twelve years old when he died the first time. He strapped an old woman to the floor of the studios garage and ran over her legs, listening to the crunch and crack of brittle bones. The post-production house would insert the screams later but Robert had no problem imagining them.

The story of the film wasn't anything to really write home about. Crone had dusted off an old script, one he had put together years before. Random acts of violence being visited upon ostensibly normal, average Americans would translate to millions at the drive-in. Who wouldn't go and see the awful potential fates that all Americans shared, shivering in their cars and cathartically screaming at the fate of the dead head cast. In all its gory glory, *All-American Horror* would show the world the terror of simply living and Robert Crone would be a millionaire. Even despite the mediocre script.

It was that mediocre script, though, that proved to be Crone's undoing. Writing in 1964 in a booze and pot-fueled haze, *All-American Horror* was dutifully scooped up by Marlene after getting Crone into the shower and sent off to the Writer's Guild for registration. The Guild registration automatically renewed each year with a rubber stamp and a check from Marlene, she did this for all Robert's scripts, and that included 1968. So, when the film went into production, Marlene submitted the report to the Guild and corresponding authorities. Marlene was incredibly efficient, after all.

Crone fell asleep in his office, content and happy for the first time in many months. He had released the cast and crew for their eight hour break. They had an eight a.m. call time and he wanted to get back to it fast. As Crone slumbered, though, Hollywood did not.

In a rare move, the International Brotherhood of Electrical Workers Local 45 in a rare team-up with United Scenic

Artists Local 829 sent three members each to visit Crone's studio. In an effort to fly fast and free, Crone didn't utilize any union labor. Not a one. Not the Screen Actors Guild, International Society of Cinematographers… no one. The rough stuff fell to the IBEW and USC. The electricians enjoyed the help from their set design and lighting brethren and after the tip from the Writer's Guild it was a forgone conclusion: *All-American Horror* needed to be shut down.

The big secret about the film was still a little cloudy and the usual crowbar and fire ax entrance method to the rear of the studio resulted in a pretty bad scene. Hell bent on breaking lights and cameras, the union members did not expect to walk, literally, into a pack of 20 dead heads who were not so patiently waiting for their close-up.

The undead tore into the electricians, gaffers, best boys, grips, scene painters, set designers and the rest. Most of them had laughed at one point over a beer or two about how this town would eat you alive if you didn't manage to get into the union. Luckily, the dead couldn't taste the irony and once they chewed their way through the invading force, they stepped out into the night and around sides of the building and heading for the front office.

The screams, shouts, and moans rocked Crone awake. He sat straight up and knew, just knew, that some shit had hit the fan. Maybe it was some kind of preternatural sixth sense developed as he swindled and scratched for film budgets, but he knew something was wrong.

Unfortunately for Crone, he figured it out just a minute too late. The door to the front office burst in and standing before him were the stars of *All-American Horror*. Crone swallowed hard and looked around. There was only one way in or out. This was it.

The cast lurched forward and Crone ran to the corner of the office. Every evening they would drag the Panavision into the office for safekeeping instead of keeping it on the set. He pulled it out, got it turned on and made sure there was a full mag loaded.

With a deep breath, Crone stepped forward and in front of the camera. He made sure there was enough light to register an image and he had just enough time to raise his arms as the first of the dead heads dove into him.

"Action..." Crone managed to gasp out as the others joined in. They feasted like Crone was craft service accompanied by the whir of the camera.

VARIETY REPORTED THAT *ALL-AMERICAN HORROR* GROSSED nearly three million dollars upon its wide open release in the United States. Producer Marlene Simmons was quoted praising the films auteur, Robert Crone, in a press release. She said, "He gave everything to this film and we're just happy we could honor his memory with its release."

Simmons has signed on to produce three sequels and there has been some interest from Charlton Heston to take over the role of Robert Crone.

BARBARIANS!

THE SAVAGE SWORD OF KING CONRAD

Often times, it is the beginning of a man that determines their manliness. Many more times than not, the beginning of a man was forgotten. The early years, the developmental years... the time before the manliest of men have reached their full potential are overshadowed by the hymen-busting adventures of swarthy and courageous adults. Verily, yes, we sing songs and tell tales of the exploits of manly men. Each of us normal, simple males (nothing more than a counterpart to the female of the species) lives vicariously through the aggrandized exploits of our heroes... but these stories are notoriously bereft of the beginning. How were our heroes created? What exploits put them on a path of greatness?

Gather 'round, travelers, for the seldom told beginning of a real man, a man's man, is nothing to scoff at. Do not think, for one moment, that this tale will be heard again in your lifetime for only once in a very great while does a lowly story-teller find the courage and determination to relate the beginning of King Conrad! For even telling of the things that King Conrad has done is enough to kill one who is not stout of heart and sour of drink and, lest this take my life, please tell my wife that I really, truly, believed her fellatio skills were sub-par. Cancel that last part if I happen to live.

King Conrad was conceived in the white leather backseat of a 1959 Chevy. His father, the nameless sod, was nothing special. No more a manly man than King Conrad's mother, the scientific community has been perplexed for years over the genetic leaps that King Conrad must have been able to accomplish in order to become who he is. Legend has it, though, that even as a small spermatozoa, King Conrad remembers the exact moment of his conception and, since he is always accurate, the following 'perfect storm' resulted in a milksop of a man, and a frump of a woman, combining to create the ultimate male specimen.

Soon after his birth, erupting from the womb in a showery spray of placenta and embryonic fluid, the young King warbled at the top of his lungs after the perfunctory slap from the attending physician. This being King Conrad, the newborn eyes shot open, blazing with a fury unmatched since the days of the Vikings or the savage attempts at geno-cide made by the original Pilgrims, and affixed on the doctor's offending right hand. With a skill that takes the samurai and ninja lifetimes to perfect, young King Conrad looped the still partially-filled umbilical cord around the doctor's hand and tightened it, pulling with all his might. Inordinately strong for being slightly over two minutes old, King Conrad managed to crush tendon, muscle and bone in the wrist, causing the doctor's right hand to curl up and resemble the talon of a crow. The doctor has never recovered the full use of that hand and is, currently, a dishwasher at a Golden Corral in Fresno. He is addicted to meth and weeps, with great, retching sobs, whenever he sees a child under two years old.

King Conrad, still only slightly dependent on his unflattering parents for sustenance and shelter, allowed them to live with him as long as they remained useful. To their credit, the parents of King Conrad did remain useful, doting on the tiny lord. Choosing to suckle at the breast, King Conrad would drain his mother's teats on a daily basis, wringing the sweet mother's milk from them like a tube of toothpaste. Her breasts, formerly attractive, if small, soon resembled a pair of nude-colored nylons carrying $20 in nickels. King Conrad did feel an inkling of attachment to the dour couple and would never turn them out. Due to that, he fancied himself a hopeless romantic.

King Conrad's third grade teacher, Ms. Ogyny, was the lucky recipient of the young King's attention. King Conrad reached puberty at the age of nine. Although no one, aside from Ms. Ogyny, was present at the time, legend has it that when King Conrad's testicles dropped, they smacked the floor and rattled windows. At that moment, Ms. Ogyny was in the middle of a parent/teacher conference with King Conrad (his parents were not allowed to attend) and explaining the importance of proper citizenship and sharing to the young royal. The pheromones released as King Conrad rushed headfirst into adulthood were so overpowering, Ms. Ogyny promptly resigned from her position and pledged her fealty to the young man. Although it has never been confirmed, that parent teacher conference was said to have been the moment that the former teacher earned the nickname "Future Hero Dumpster."

Unwilling to remain trapped in the same grade school that other, normal, children needed to attend, King Conrad and his concubine promptly tested out of grade school, scored perfectly on the SAT in order to attend college, and enrolled in a prestigious Ivy League school that can no longer be named due to ongoing litigation.

This is where King Conrad rose to his potential. Here, at

university, King Conrad finally faced a foe worthy of his intellect and prowess. Now twelve-years-old, King Conrad came face to face with the leader of a powerful cult of spirit worshippers that wished to deny King Conrad his rightful excesses of drink, concubines and amoral behavior. This leader was named Father O'Malley and believed King Conrad nothing more than a simple child to be assimilated into the cult (that would meet off campus every Wednesday for something called Student Mass) and have his burgeoning awesomeness replaced with automaton-thinking that plagued the other group members.

O'Malley and Conrad met on accident, really. After thoroughly demolishing his final exam in Advanced Particle Physics, and thoroughly demolishing his physics professor's vagina, King Conrad was in a fairly good mood... for him. He had decided, due to the triumphs of the day, to forgo his plans for mounting an attack on the Tappa Pi sorority wherein he had planned to replenish his concubine horde with fresh, nubile young co-eds, and spend a quiet evening at home with Ms. Ogyny. She had performed admirably over the years and had firmly entrenched herself into King Conrad's heart. This would pass for love, probably, to a normal human but the boiling rage that fueled King Conrad would only allow this affection to be called 'un-hate.' He un-hated Ms. Ogyny and she was a loyal companion.

So, with thoughts of a mani-pedi on his mind, and a growler of stout ale calling his name, the still-young king literally ran into Father O'Malley.

The good father tipped the scales at nearly 300 pounds and this looked like an upside-down ice cream cone on his five foot frame. Seeing eye to eye with the young king, Father O'Malley smiled, his greasy jowls bending and arching to accommodate the unfamiliar action.

"I beg your pardon, young man, don't you have any

manners? I am a priest, after all!" The father said, refusing to step to the side.

Although unfamiliar with the black uniform and odd white collar, King Conrad knew this type all too well. An air of false authority surrounded the man and it took all of the king's strength to not draw his sword and find out just how much belly fat there stood between him and the man's vital organs.

"You would do well to step to the side, glutton! I move for no man!" King Conrad announced to the porcine preacher. The king's fiery glare caused the Fat Friar to shrink backward for a moment, realizing that he was far, far outmatched in battle of strengths and wits.

Collecting himself, the priest reached into a pocket, most likely shoving aside a donut or some other baked treat, and pulled a book out. He held it to his chest, somehow finding strength in clutching it. The obese man stood tall, looking over King Conrad's head (he was still unable to look him in the eye).

"I am Father O'Malley of The Blessed Virgin! You, dear boy, have been possessed by the devil! The impertinence! The rage! I shall exorcise your demons!"

Father O'Malley cried this out and, without hesitating, grabbed King Conrad in a large bear hug. Caught off guard, for the first time ever, King Conrad could only stare at Father O'Malley, dumbstruck and caught up in the fat man's clutches. The king had never been surprised before, in all reality, and the last time he was physically assaulted was his birth. So, naturally, although magnificent, he was unused to such behavior.

King Conrad came to his senses quickly, though. Father O'Malley could not have held the king longer than thirty seconds before a disproportionately small erection poked King Conrad in the navel. One could only imagine the level of Father O'Malley's desire needed to imbue his penis with enough power to actually move his massive belly and strike King Conrad in the belly button.

Both the priest and the king's eyes grew wide in shock. This took but a moment. Then, regaining his senses, King Conrad used his near-Herculean strength to break the hold of Father O'Malley.

The priest's arms flailed and he fell backwards, falling on his cushioned rear, as King Conrad stood over him. Hands balled into fists and eyes burning with rage, he towered over the mewling, sweating preacher.

"No one dares to violate the navel of King Conrad!" The king growled through clenched teeth. With each breath, his anger grew and the king reached for his Jansport backpack. Inside, a short sword lay nestled between the remnants of the lunch that Ms. Ogyny had packed for him and his World Civilizations textbook.

Seeing the king move for the backpack, Father O'Malley scuttled backward on his rear, hoping to put as much space as possible between the king and himself. From within another, deeper, pocket, Father O'Malley retrieved a small metallic cross. He grinned, lasciviously, as he held it out in front of himself.

King Conrad stopped, unsure of how to proceed. Was this some kind of weapon?

"I am not alone, boy-warrior! I have many, many souls… my flock… and they will do my bidding!" The said this quickly and, with that, turned the cross around and shoved the end in his mouth. Father O'Malley's cheeks puffed out as if he were blowing some kind of instrument, yet King Conrad could hear no sound.

Of course, the king surmised a few moments later, he wasn't supposed to hear a sound. The small metallic cross was nothing more than a cleverly disguised sheep-whistle! From behind trees, out of shadows, emerging from doors, people streamed. King Conrad lost count quickly enough as the hordes streamed around him. They did not touch him, but surrounded the fat priest, keeping the king from getting to his foe.

Although blocked from view now, surrounded by the huddled mass, Father O'Malley moved away from King Conrad in relative safety.

"Coward! Face me!" the king called out.

From within the retreating mass of cultists, the Father exclaimed, "We will meet again, King Conrad! We will meet and I will show you my holy sepulcher! Dirty little boys need to be punished!"

King Conrad fumed as the undulating mass of flesh keeping him from his prey retreated into the distance.

With grim countenance, the boy-king looked to the sky and squinted against the setting sun. He knew the path to take now, the only path. Father O'Malley would rue the day his purple-headed warrior poked King Conrad in the belly. He would bring the fight to the fat man and, by all the gods, he would smite the quivering glob of gelatin down in front of his flock.

A grin crossed King Conrad's face. A master tactician, naturally, he had already begun to form a plan. Maybe the Tappa Pi sorority would be receiving a visit tonight after all.

FATHER O'MALLEY BLESSED HIS PERSONAL ALTAR OVER and over again until the palm of his holy hand bled, stigmata-like. He knew, in his heart of hearts, that he would meet this King Conrad again. This heathen that dared to lay unwanted hands on one of the Divine's Chosen would pay!

Father O'Malley smiled as he wrapped gauze around the friction wounds of his right hand and limbered up his left.

Just thinking of the revenge he would visit on King Conrad, Father O'Malley's 'hornless Triceratops' leapt to attention, ready to spray down the private altar one more time with the holy seed.

O'Malley grasped his penis but, before he could begin, a resounding crash echoed through the church. O'Malley's quarters were located in the rear, quite a distance from where the unwashed masses worshipped, and yet, he could feel the power of the explosion, or whatever it was, rattle its way through the entire complex.

Stuffing his penis back in his pants, O'Malley rushed from his room to see what kind of devil-spawned catastrophe would dare visit itself upon this church! His church!

The jiggly mass of flesh didn't have to wait long. O'Malley burst into the rectory and was graced with a sight that he, or no other God-fearing man, would soon forget.

Before him, riding a on a chariot comprised of naked college co-eds, rode King Conrad. His twelve-year-old body clad only in a loincloth, muscles defined and ripped far beyond the tender years flexed and pulled the reins. Before trampling Father O'Malley, the sorority chariot skidded to a halt, the lead sisters' double D breasts swinging in protest.

Father O'Malley squealed in abject horror. First and foremost, a barbarian king, large sword raised in the air, just rode into his church on the backs of supplicant nude women. Secondly, this was the first time that the priest had ever seen adult female genitalia and it frightened him beyond reason, like some kind of Lovecraftian Cosmic Beast made real.

"Defiler of youth!" King Conrad bellowed at the priest, "Prepare to be smitten!"

O'Malley fumbled, hands under his cassock. He managed to pull the whistle-fix from its hiding place, but it never made it to his lips.

A scream, shrill and feral from above, caused O'Malley to

panic, dropping the lifeline to his flock of minions. He looked up just in time to see a half-naked woman, older than the co-eds, dropping from the ceiling. She landed on O'Malley's head and wrapped her legs around his neck, continuing to wail a fierce battle cry.

King Conrad laughed and pointed at the gasping priest with his sword.

"Fat man, meet Ms. Ogyny... my tutor!" King Conrad said. He leapt down from this chick chariot and strode over to the incapacitated priest. Kneeling, King Conrad came face to face with the purple-tinged padre.

"Before you succumb to the vicious legs of Ms. Ogyny, remember one thing... your humiliation will hold no bounds and it comes at..." At this point, King Conrad stood, for full dramatic effect, and raised his sword in the air, Frazetta-style. The coeds broke ranks, as if called by a testosterone siren, and wrapped themselves around the legs of the manly monarch. Only then did Conrad finish his sentence. He bellowed, "The Savage Sword of King Conrad!"

Father O'Malley's vision blurred and he succumbed.

VISITORS TO THE PERPETUAL VISION OF THE BLESSED Virgin's Wednesday evening mass were greeted with a lawn ornament that would probably never make the "best of" list in *Better Church and Papacy* magazine. Trussed up, sans cassock, Father O'Malley rolled on the front lawn of the church very much alive and unable to stand. His hands had been tied behind his back. The flaccid shaft of his purple-helmeted warrior featured a knotted rope that ran to just between the third and fourth chins and encircled his neck. Hog-tied, for lack of a better term. This effectively caused the large father's little member to be pulled, stretched and yanked the more he struggled. Due to his large size, in order just to breathe, O'Malley was required to move around quite a bit.

Shaved into the man's back was a message. It read: "Here be your false idol." Pinned through O'Malley's chest, a large flier finished the sentiment. It read: "Never more will unholy consummation of flesh between portly faith deceivers and innocents be condoned on this campus, in this kingdom. So decrees King Conrad!"

MAD SCIENCE!

PEGGED

1 THIS LITTLE PIGGY WENT TO MARKET

Peter Adelman knew, just knew, he was a freak. That was it and there wasn't anything that anyone could do about it. He hid his shame, of course, and went about his daily life as well as he possibly could. But it weighed on him. It weighed on him heavily and, under that weight, even Peter's physical appearance changed. He lost weight, making his military school uniform baggy. He stooped like an old man as if that burden rested squarely on his shoulders, making him look like a returning soldier that had seen too much action. It wasn't like he could stop his freakish nature or make the thoughts quit running through his head. They were there, ever present, from morning till night. And they were heavy. Unfortunately, there was nothing that Peter could do and no one he could tell. What would his peers think? What would his superiors think? At seventeen, Peter Adelman, military high school senior, knew that he was a podophiliac. Although he was a full letter away from being a child molester, Peter had an unquenchable desire, longing for and addiction to human feet. He possessed a foot fetish that, he felt, possessed him right back.

In doing some clandestine research on his own condition, Peter found that there are two types of foot fetishes. The first is rather benign and deals with an overly zealous appreciation of the aesthetics of the foot. It is not sexual. What Peter was saddled with, though, was the second, more serious form of fetishism. Feet aroused him. The thought of feet instilled in him an insatiable desire to touch, caress and fondle feet. He loved the smell of feet and used shoes. The silver-lining, at least to Peter, was that his predilection had limits. Definite limits. He was encouraged by the fact that male feet did nothing for him. Sweaty, hairy, sasquatch-esque feet were not a turn on.

The ladies, on the other hand, were his cup of tea. On those rare occasions during his young life where he had been able to touch, even briefly, a woman's foot, Peter had to leave the room quickly before his raging erection and imminent orgasm gave him away. This was the burden he was under, the hidden shame. If anyone knew, he would be ostracized and reviled --labeled a freak and treated like a pariah. He would never be able to bear that kind of shunning. It was simply too great. Tortured, Peter sloughed through life from one mundane moment to the next, avoiding women in general, and feet in particular, as he tried to keep his aberration in check. It was a horrid existence.

He, of course, blamed his mother.

Peter wasn't sure exactly how a paraphilia of this nature started. Aberrant sexual behavior had to have a root somewhere, right? Growing up in a strict Methodist home, Peter surmised, didn't help matters.

His father, Teddy Adelman, was a wishy-washy man. Short, slight of build, balding and desperately clinging onto a woefully inadequate mustache, he was one of hundreds of accountants in a massive firm. Teddy crunched numbers all day, acquiescing to whatever mid-level management stoolie happened to pass his cubicle. Teddy was lucky enough to attend a Methodist church (because that is what he was supposed to do) and, after being badgered into volunteering for one of the church's pancake breakfast events, he managed to meet Betty Jo Slocum.

Betty Jo, the daughter of the former minister of Holy Grace United Methodist Church, was an active member of the church despite her father's uneremonious firing amid allegations of fraud, graft, and sexual misconduct. No one took the sexual misconduct charges seriously, though. At a United Methodist Church looking at the back of a young woman's leg for too long could be considered sexual misconduct. He was guilty as hell, though, on the fraud and graft charges. Charlie Slocum made a mint, was fired and disappeared.

This made Betty Jo a little angry. She was the exact opposite of Teddy. Snide, domineering, opinionated, tall (nearing six feet) and obese (she preferred portly), Betty Jo had problems making friends even if they didn't know about her family. Her devotion to God was so true, she believed, that He would deliver to her the perfect man and perfect mate. Unfortunately for Betty Jo, He waited until she was 38 years old. He had given her Teddy who was, quite possibly, the only man on the planet that could be married to her.

Teddy had no backbone. He was an invertebrate that lived under the iron will of his wife. Betty Jo ruled that home as a dictator, just like her father had ruled her childhood home (and the church). The Adelmans attended church more than regularly, praying to God every day that they would be blessed with a child.

Miraculously, on the eve of her 39th birthday, Betty Jo Adelman gave birth to Peter Adelman. He was a bit premature and small due to the age of his mother, mostly, but Peter gutted it out and survived those important first 48 hours. Betty Jo, and Teddy (because he had to), just knew that Peter was a miracle.

The other members of the church also considered the birth of Peter to be a miracle. They whispered about it. It was a miracle that Betty Jo got someone to marry her. It was a miracle that Teddy could actually 'perform' in the bedroom with her constant badgering. It was a miracle that she didn't eat the poor man after conceiving like some giant, pudgy praying mantis.

The ladies club at the church just knew that she guided Teddy's obviously anemic sperm to her voracious ovaries through a sheer force of will.

Regardless, Peter was alive! And, over the course of his childhood, he would wish he was never born over and over again.

The problems for Peter really didn't begin, as far as he could remember, until he was five or six years old. His father, playing the dutiful employee (at work and at home) had absolutely no say in his upbringing. This wasn't uncommon, per se, but Betty Jo's particular brand of child-rearing could have been considered disconcerting by some and outright horrendous by others. The Methodists were still making up their minds about spoiling the rod, or what even constituted the rod.

At an early age, around five or six as indicated, Peter distinctly remembered that his mother stepped on his testicles as a form of punishment. As a young boy, there wasn't much to punish down there but the agony of a full grown woman (overly grown) smashing her toes onto her son's testicles had to have been excruciating. Peter remembered the pain faintly, but the feelings of helplessness and shame were all too real.

Oddly, there was no build up, no testing phase in regard to Betty Jo's behavior. One day, she did not step on her son's testicles and the next day she did. A switch flipped or a synapse fired or something happened and, suddenly, she ground her toes into her son's balls for even the most minor of infractions.

When "Lay down!" cut through the air, Peter knew what came next. Although the pain and discomfort were terrible, Peter believed that all little boys lived this way. It was just how you were punished for being naughty. His father had never balked at the punishment and his mother acted as if there wasn't anything wrong. This continued for many years, but took a drastic turn when Peter turned ten-years-old.

Peter, through his schooling and talking to other fifth graders realized, quite suddenly one day, that a boy's mother shouldn't be stepping on his scrotum on a near-daily basis. Oh, he hid his questions in jokes and laughter, to gauge what his school friends might say, but Peter found out in short order that his mother was *wrong*. She was *bad* and that this was *abuse*. Those three words that he would never dare utter in his mother's presence were the only things that ran through his mind. Every mash, every squash and every aching moment of punishment rushed back to the young boy and he became ill.

He returned home to find his mother occupied with cooking dinner. He made no fuss, held his emotions in check, and patiently waited for his father to arrive. Peter knew that his father was, essentially, useless but faced with the knowledge that his son was being abused, in horrible ways, had to get Teddy Adelman to spring into action. Maybe his dad just didn't know that squishing a boy's scrotum wasn't an awful, harmful and sadistic punishment. Peter would make him see and once his dad found out, well, things would change.

Peter heard the old Corolla pull into the driveway and the door shut. Peter sprung from his bed, down the stairs, and arrived just in time to help his father off with same grey overcoat he had been wearing for twenty years and the same briefcase that had carried, and would only carry, a brown paper bag lunch.

"Thanks, son," Teddy said. He was appreciative of the boy. No one ever paid Teddy Adelman much mind. This was a change. "Where's your mother?"

Peter looked at the carpet, afraid to even breathe for a moment. "Cooking dinner."

Teddy sighed. Good. If she was occupied she wouldn't be badgering him. He smiled. Teddy and Peter stood in awkward silence for a moment. They weren't used to this, Betty Jo usually did the talking.

Peter gathered his courage and said, "Can I talk to you for a minute... alone?"

Teddy was taken aback. He never expected this, despite being the boy's father for the last ten years. He smiled, genuinely, the first time in a long time, and wrapped his arm around Peter's shoulders. "Sure," Teddy said. "Let's go out to the patio."

On the patio, once the pair had been seated, Peter took a deep breath. He began telling his father about the ball squishing and, before Peter knew it, the words flowed out of his mouth and into the ether. He spoke quickly, but at length, regaling his father with instance after instance of ritual abuse. Finally, after detailing the last, horrific, episode, Peter ran out of words and fell silent.

Through the entire monologue, Teddy Adelman's face never changed. He listened, watching his son intently. He was the dutiful father then, mouth a serious slit, gauging what the issue was and how he could help. When Peter finished, Teddy placed a hand on his son's shoulder and took a deep breath.

"Have you told your mother that you… don't like this?" Teddy asked.

Peter shook his head. That would have been a death sentence.

"Good. Let's keep this between us, OK?"

Peter's shoulders slumped. His father had failed him again. Peter was on the verge of tears when the stillness on the patio was rent asunder with a shriek.

Peter and his father leapt up from the lounge chairs to find Betty Jo standing near the patio door. She was breathing in large, heavy gasps like a bull about to charge. She lifted a rolling pin and pointed it at the two men in her life.

Instinctively, Teddy pulled Peter in front of him and pushed him toward Betty Jo. "It was all him, honey! I didn't have anything to do with it!"

Betty Jo glared at them, her eyes like lasers, and Peter felt as if they were blazing into his brain, heating his whole head up.

"You think I'm abusing, you?" Betty Jo asked.

Teddy shook his head, he knew better.

Peter took a deep breath and gathered every ounce of courage he possessed. He nodded his head. Expecting another terrifying screech, despite Teddy's traitorous act, father and son clung to each other.

Betty Jo just smiled. "Oh. Well, I guess I better really abuse you, then, so you know the difference."

Before Peter realized what had happened, both he and his father were forced to the ground, sans pants. Each of them spread eagle and lay parallel to one another. Neither Peter nor his father moved eyes or head to catch a glimpse of the other. There was no commiserating, there was only Betty Jo.

After what seemed like a thousand years, Betty Jo stepped

into the room. She was wearing a bathing suit and no shoes, of course. Without a word, she stepped over to Teddy and nudged his scrotum with her toe. At the slightest touch, Teddy's flaccid penis jumped, bouncing in anticipation. Before Teddy's member could fill out, Betty Jo mashed down on his scrotum with her toes.

Clenching and unclenching her toes caused Teddy to howl in pain but, as Peter listened, he heard his father cry out in what sounded like joy, rapture and, if he would have had the vocabulary, he may have thought 'ecstasy.'

Betty Jo moaned and quaked as she kneaded her husband's balls, rolling the testicles against the floor and bringing them just to the point of bursting before drawing back and simply kneading them more.

Teddy's howls of pain and pleasure increased in volume and intensity, building to a crescendo. With a little more pressure, a little more gut-wrenching pain, we would explode…

Betty Jo quit right there. She stepped off of Teddy's scrotum and stood back. He moaned, desperate for those toes to once again nearly destroy his manhood.

Teddy's anguished bleats were an aphrodisiac to Betty Jo. His torment was her satisfaction and she nearly came listening to her husband weep. She looked over to Peter and licked her lips.

She stepped to Peter and he knew what was going to happen next. They had been through this many times before, but never like this. The room was charged; it was electric. Peter's father sobbed softly to himself nearby. Betty Jo shook as she hovered her foot over Peter's scrotum. He gritted his teeth, waiting for the intense pain to begin, like getting punched over and over again in the stomach.

Betty Jo stepped down, pressing her foot onto her son's

testicles, showing him that he was better off keeping his big mouth shut.

A strangled cry escaped Peter as he felt his mother's toes knead into his balls, rolling them on the floor, pressing them like martini olives with just enough pressure to threaten the pimento when the strangest thing happened. The pain was as intense as anything else he could imagine and, after working all day, his mother's feet smelled like sweat and vinyl shoes. Whether it was the smell, or the pressure, or the situation, he didn't know. Peter had been told, in school, what was happening but had never experienced that particular event until today. As his mother stepped on his scrotum, Peter Adelman got his first erection.

Betty Jo watched it grow, wide-eyed. Shocked and unable to move, Betty Jo could only stand there as her son's pre-pubescent erection mocked her. She had no intention of creating another Teddy Adelman. There is no way she could abide another weak-willed, spineless man to walk the face of this planet. She stepped off of Peter's scrotum, thoughts of her own pleasure forgotten.

She stared down at her son, his tiny erection waggling at her like an accusatory finger. She glared at the boy, straddling his chest and hovering over him.

"You disgust me!" she said, spitting as she said it.

Peter, confused, finally looked over at his father, hoping that, this one time, he could do something. Teddy looked up at Betty Jo, paying his son no mind, and whimpered.

"I… I'm sorry!" Peter stammered. He stood and put his underwear back on. He backed into the corner of the room, trying desperately to distance himself.

Betty Jo just watched her son back away. She did not follow.

"Just like your father. You're sick, Peter… sick!" And,

with that, she turned and marched out of the room. Teddy followed on his knees, begging for one more chance.

Peter slid to the floor more perplexed than ever. He did not know what to do. Questions whipped through his mind like a tornado. Who could he tell? What was happening to him? Was he really like his father? The one question that he couldn't even come close to articulating, the one that just sat there, in the back of his mind, festering, was the question that he wanted answered the most: Would she do it again?

Peter never found out. The next morning he was shipped off to the DeMarcus Military School for Wayward Youths where he would spend the next eight years in relative isolation from his family.

2 THIS LITTLE PIGGY STAYED HOME

Peter found the military school to his liking, at first. The fifth grade finished out at DeMarcus and he moved on to the sixth grade, growing taller and stronger. As he aged, though, his thoughts turned more and more frequently to his mother. He was glad to be rid of her, no doubt, and his father, too, but he couldn't stop thinking of her. More specifically, he couldn't stop thinking about her feet. He knew it was wrong, but he got an electric charge… a thrill out of thinking about how her toes felt, buried in his scrotum. The warm, moist feel of them on his skin got his motor going and remembering the smell of those feet, unbound after a sweaty day in vinyl shoes, was intoxicating. That constituted the majority of Peter's daydreams for years. It caused Peter no end of heartache and private shame, but he couldn't help himself.

Fortunately for him, the instances of actually having to interact with a female and, by attachment, a female foot was relatively slim at DeMarcus. Until, of course, he reached the tenth grade. He was a strapping lad of fourteen and beginning what non-military students considered the second year of high school. At the DeMarcus Military School for Wayward Youths, the tenth grade was the year that cadets branched off into different areas of expertise. Unusually adept at mathematics and design, Peter went into drafting and science programs that were heavy on arithmetic and physical sciences. In so doing, he was placed in the class of Major Henderson. Major Margaret Henderson.

And then there was the puberty issue.

The first 'change of life' was upon Peter. He had grown tall, nearing six feet already, and was thin. Strong, unlike his father, and kind, unlike his mother, he was relatively popular. Without a real parental figure to take his concerns too, all of Peter's knowledge regarding puberty was from the television and older boys... not the greatest avenues of information. So, as hair sprouted from unusual areas and movement without causing an erection became a near impossibility, Peter was forced to sit and watch one of the most beautiful women he had ever seen, including on television, lecture his class each day about geometry, physics, and spatial relations. Even when the spatial relations within Peter's uniform pants became uncomfortable.

Major Henderson wasn't tall, but she was brunette, her hair fashioned into a tight bun while she taught. She wore a uniform as well and had begun her tenure at DeMarcus after a stint in the United States Marine Corps. Everything about her was perfectly placed. Her uniform shirt, tight around a large bosom, had its buttons perfectly centered and ending in the gig line, or middle, of the belt buckle. Her DeMarcus-issued skirt was pressed and clean every day. Peter felt she was a bit old-fashioned since she wore panty hose (the kind with a dark band down the back, even). He would appraise her like this, every day, from top to bottom, always ending on her shiny black pumps, buffed and gleaming. Whenever

Peter looked at those shoes, he sighed and blood rushed from his head to other, important areas. He could imagine the smell, nylon rubbing against toes all day... toes that could knead and crush and... Peter would snap out of the daydream before anything sticky happened, but a few times it had been a close call. Regardless, he managed to survive the attentions of the attentive and beautiful Major Henderson.

A few months into the tenth grade and it all came crashing down. In the normal course of life at DeMarcus, Peter would attend class and then go onto whatever work patrol he had drawn. For the second half of the winter term, Peter was responsible for cleaning the pool area. DeMarcus did not have a swim team so the pool was seldom used and Peter performed his perfunctory duties automatically.

During mid-terms, though, the faculty often spent a great deal more time at the school, prepping and grading. This held true for Major Henderson and, in order to take a quick break and relax, she walked into the pool area carrying a gym bag. Peter, lost in thoughts of painted toenails, snapped out of his reverie with the clack of Major Henderson's shoes meeting tile.

He spun around to find the Major heading right for him. He stood his ground, mainly out of fear, mouth agape, nearly dropping the pool skimming net.

"Cadet, where is the locker room?" she asked.

Peter just stared. This was the first time a woman had spoken to him outside of a classroom in some time. Blood rushed south.

"Mr. Adelma, I'm speaking to you. Where is the locker room?"

Peter shook enough of the shock off to point in the direction of the locker rooms.

The Major looked over and nodded.

"Good. I don't suppose there are separate male and females locker rooms?"

Peter shook his head.

"Then you need to stand guard while I change. You can manage that, can't you?"

Peter nodded his head. He could only imagine those breasts, the flat, fit abdomen, the legs and… Peter dared not think it.

Major Henderson nodded, spun on her high heels, and marched into the locker room. Peter followed behind and turned at the door, holding the net in front of him like some kind of spear.

As he stood at the door, he could hear Henderson changing. She hummed a tune he didn't know, but it sounded like music from an angel's trumpet. Two dull thuds as Henderson kicked her shoes off sent a chill up Peter's spine. His lip quivered and a cold sweat broke out from his shoulders and down his back. The rustle of clothes, a zipper, elastic slapping into place. Peter held his knees together as the soft slap of bare feet on tile echoed as it moved closer.

Major Henderson, now sporting a modest, aqua blue one piece bathing suit, breezed past Peter without so much as turning her head.

"Thank you, Cadet," she said and padded to the edge of the pool's deep end.

Peter eyes were wide at the site of them. The pair of them. Her feet. The Major's heels were yellowed, a bit callused from her choice of footwear and he could see where bunions were beginning to form. He nails were painted olive green, of course, but it was her toes the drove him wild. They were long and slender, with the second toe just slightly longer than the big toe. He imagined them like that. From this distance, he couldn't smell her feet but the chlorine would ruin that soon enough.

Major Henderson squatted and stretched her arms out, preparing to dive. The veins running alongside her ankles protruded and the tips of her toes turned white as she rocked onto them, ready to leap.

Peter's groin strained against his pants. He watched the muscles in her feet tense and then, suddenly, she sprung into the air. Peter exhaled, blowing the air out with such force he nearly double over. As he had watched her, he had forgotten to breathe.

In the water, Major Henderson kicked and stroked, working on laps from one end of the small pool to the other. The churning water obscured her feet and the voyeur in Peter had his hopes dashed. And then a brainstorm. Why watch?

Peter reasoned that Major Henderson didn't have a locker and, therefore, she would have no place to put her clothes. With a quick glance to the pool to make sure she was still swimming, Peter dropped the skimming net and slipped into the locker room.

The green, sickly, overhead lights gave the locker room scurvy, but they were bright and it didn't take Peter long to find the neatly laid out uniform of Major Henderson on a bench and, below it, the Holy Grail.

Peter kneeled before the high-heeled shoes (not high enough to be fashionable, but still business-like) and lifted one up. He carefully pulled the wadded nylon from the shoe. Like some magic trick, the single stocking went on and on, finally ending as the footie of the stocking popped free. Shaking like a leaf, Peter rubbed the foot of the nylon against his cheek. His body shook in pleasure, this simple act bringing him so much satisfaction he nearly wept. Peter smiled knowing that this was just the appetizer.

Peter flung the stocking over his shoulder and held the shiny, black shoe in both hands. He trembled as he brought the shoe to his face and held it right below his nose. He shut his eyes and sniffed. Long and deep. Major Henderson's musk erupted through his nostrils. The smell of a foot trapped in leather, surrounded by nylon all day, washed over Peter and he fell backwards, onto this posterior as joyous spasms wracked his body. He convulsed in sheer pleasure, never pulling the shoe away from his face. He kept it there, ensuring that Major Henderson's scent would stay with him as long as possible.

He longed to crawl into the shoe and sleep, safe and sound, until Major Henderson, or his mother, even, would come for it. He would need to be punished then. Peter imagined those olive green-tipped toes stepping on his testicles, rolling each one...

"Cadet!"

Peter's eyes shot open, wide as saucers. Standing before him, towel in hand, was Major Henderson. The two of them just stared at one another, unmoving. Peter continued to hold her shoe aloft, raging erection tenting his pants. Major Henderson clutched her towel and dripped pool water onto the floor of the locker room. It was so quiet in there, the drops sounded like gunshots.

Finally, Major Henderson broke the silence.

"I suggest, Mr. Adelman, that you put my footwear down, immediately."

Peter complied instantly. As he stood, he became aware of his own compromising appendage and bent over, trying to hide it from his teacher.

"I'm sorr..." he began.

The Major cut him off before he could begin. "Go. Now. I won't speak of this and you will never tell a soul, do you understand me?"

Peter nodded as he hunched, still pathetically trying to hide his boner from Major Henderson. He turned to leave but Henderson stopped him.

"Wait a minute. Tomorrow, in class, none of this happened." The Major said. Then, she scowled. Her lips pulled back in disgust and she looked Peter up and down. "You should know, Mr. Adelman, that what you are is a freak. A deviant, bastard freak. I understand that your family may have messed you up a bit, but you're smart. You're bright. You have a future. Right now, today, whatever you think you were doing compromised that future. Do you understand?"

Peter nodded again. Henderson's disgust dissipated a bit. Her gaze softened and, with it, Peter felt some of that tightness in his groin alleviated.

"I like you, Peter. You're a bright student. If you continue to pursue this... this... I don't even know what to call it. This fetish, it will ruin you. Believe me. It is aberrant and it is unwholesome."

Peter nodded again. He turned to leave but the Major stopped him one more time. She was back to Major Henderson, no first names but no abject disgust.

"Mr. Adelman? Just for the record, and my peace of mind, you didn't...?"

"Didn't what, ma'am?"

Major Henderson looked down at her shoe and then to Peter's nether region. "How do I put this? You didn't finish in my shoe, did you?"

Peter's eyes grew wide again. He shook is head vehemently. "No, no ma'am. I... I... would never... I mean, never try..."

She silenced him again with a hand. "Good. Thank you. Please leave while I change."

Peter nodded and shot out of the locker room. He snatched up the skimming net as he left and scurried to the opposite end of the pool area, backing into a corner.

Eventually, changed, Major Henderson left the locker

room. For the briefest of moments their eyes met as she marched through the area and toward the main campus. That look was the period on the conversation. It said freak. It said deviant. It said pervert.

Peter slumped in the corner. His mother was right and he had been found out. He trusted Major Henderson to keep quiet about everything, but he had to change. He couldn't go on like this.

THE REMAINDER OF THE SCHOOL YEAR PASSED WITHOUT incident, although Major Henderson's classes were a bit colder than they had been before. Peter tried to force the thought of the day at the pool from his mind, and was largely successful. He weakened, from time to time, and thought of that evening while he showered, or while his suite-mates were away during the holidays. That was when it was the roughest for Peter. Alone at school with no one but the cleaning staff, kitchen staff and the television made it difficult for Peter to forget about things. Like Major Henderson. Like Major Henderson's shoes.

He was unwelcome at home, so Peter decided to delve into his studies. His aptitude for drafting, mathematics and the physical sciences, along with his bizarre (at least to some of his teachers) knowledge of human anatomy from the waist down led him through the remainder of his time at DeMarcus and landed him a scholarship to the State University where he would double major in engineering and biology.

As he grew older, and more aware of just what kind of monster he had become (or, at least, it would appear to others), he found it easier to abstain from physical demonstrations of his obsession. He avoided social contact, even with other boys, and dove into his studies.

The relative anonymity of college helped Peter. He did not speak and was not spoken to outside of the classroom. Inside the classroom he performed admirably. With the ability to choose his own classes and, by extension, his own instructors he made sure that he was dealing with male faculty. He studied hard, pouring himself into his work... which served as his only outlet for that bizarre fascination of his.

From early on in college, Peter had settled on a career choice that would afford him the luxury of accessing his desires but force him to keep them at bay. He applied his engineering skill and his anatomical knowledge into the field of prosthetics. Peter's guidance academic counselors had never seen a man so driven at such a young age, who knew, without a doubt, exactly what he wanted to do for the rest of his life.

Peter's college career was uneventful. He tailored his program to the pursuit of prosthetic limb design, specializing in prosthetics that would be affixed below the knee, and graduated cum laude with the dual degree. So scarred was he from the Henderson Incident, as he called it, Peter would only occasionally glance at his fellow coeds choice of footwear or, on those warm summer days, check out how seductive flip flops could be as they spread apart large toe from the rest. Peter had formed an iron will.

His studies helped, though. By Peter's junior year, he knew every bone, tendon and fiber in the human foot and how it applied, in terms of mechanics, to the acts of walking, running, diving... anything. Quite willfully, Peter became the unheralded, and unknown, expert on the dynamics of feet and how modern prosthetics could mimic that allowing amputees, accident victims, and any other individual missing a limb a chance at a normal life.

Peter was proud of what he accomplished in school. Sure,

while studying he would have to look at images of tens of thousands of feet, videos, too. He relegated his tactile studies to corpses in the medical school cadaver lab, which were mostly men. Peter would forgive himself the occasional indiscretion, though, as he masturbated onto the feet of a dead woman… but that was it. No one would ever know and the women that paid the ultimate price before becoming scientific fodder probably didn't much care what happened to their feet.

A man's got to do what a man's got to do, Peter reasoned. So, as he walked across the stage, accepting both of his degrees, Peter was assured of his future. A job offer had come in from the Restore Institute in Arizona and Peter had accepted. He would be working with some of the finest scientific minds in the field of prosthetics, helping war vets, diabetics, children… anyone he could. Peter shook hands with the Dean, who couldn't quite place the young man. Peter smiled at his fellow classmates, who smiled back but didn't remember if they had had any classes with Peter. Finally, he smiled out to the sea of families, there to watch their child or sibling or whatever graduate. Peter knew his parents weren't there. In fact, he wasn't even sure if they were both still alive. He would show them. Success was the best revenge.

Peter smiled even wider. Yeah, he was a freak… but he would never let them see him sweat.

3 THIS LITTLE PIGGY ATE ROAST BEEF

Peter was drenched in sweat. His first week at the Restore Institute had gone swimmingly. While on the tour of the facility, he even managed to find and correct a design flaw in an artificial toe joint being developed for potential national distribution. Not only did that endear him to his new administration, but also shot Peter to the top of the heap as far as Research and Development Superstars went. He was on top of the world. His office was spacious, he had proven via his school work that he was a self-starter so there was very little oversight and Peter could spend his days designing new feet for the feetless. Except for Tuesdays.

Part of Peter's job description, that he had overlooked, included the foot auditions. This happened each Tuesday. Along with three other engineers in his department, Peter would audition feet in search of those feet that would be aesthetically pleasing enough that they could be used to cast and mold for the prosthetics that the Restore Institute developed. Peter, a very old woman named Doris and another new recruit, Lenny, were to take notes and judge the feet in front of them according to their symmetry, line, shape and overall aesthetic beauty. The best would be cast in alginate and then a mold made in order to create the resin prosthetics. The Institute had received high marks for this extra step in trying to make their patients feel as 'normal' as possible, but Peter was terrified.

He had consciously avoided looking at or touching real feet for so long, he wasn't sure what would happen. Awash in sweat, he sat in the small room with his two colleagues and downed glass after glass of water. The pedi parade had yet to begin and Peter was already dry-mouthed and having hot flashes.

Worst of all, he could feel that formerly familiar tightness in his pants again. Just the thought of a parade of feet nearly had him bursting from the seams. He tried to control his breathing and wiped his forehead with a handkerchief. He didn't know if he could control himself. His penis throbbed against the wall of his trousers.

Lenny and Doris snatched glances at Peter from time to time. Neither of them had ever had the occasion to have a conversation with Peter (Peter saw to that), but they inched away hoping to avoid whatever disease plagued Peter then.

When the door opened and the first candidate entered, Peter nearly fainted. He laughed, out loud, and sighed in relief. Lenny and Doris turned to Peter, unsure of what to do. The foot candidate, with bare feet and pant legs rolled up, stopped short.

Peter smiled and waved the man in, "I'm sorry. I… haven't been feeling too well… from a migraine, you see," Peter said, smiling the entire time. "It just went away, just now, poof!"

The model, Doris and Lenny all nodded, accepting the excuse.

Peter smiled broadly and wiped his forehead one last time. A man. It was a man! Hairy feet did nothing for Peter. He didn't know what would happen when a woman did come through (she was bound to at some point) but Peter felt that making it through this first model without an incident would set a good precedent. So, Peter gauged the man's feet for aesthetic beauty, functionality and symmetry as dispassionately as he could.

Luckily, for Peter, most of the Restore Institute's work was wrapped up in returning veterans and, up to that point, women were rarely put into combat roles so Peter found that Tuesdays were mainly used to gauge the feet of men in order to help other men… and Peter was just fine with that. Of course, the occasional woman came in to model and Peter made do. Either he left the room, letting Lenny and Doris handle it with a conveniently timed meeting or he would suffer through the ordeal using a large binder clip on his inner thigh in order to maintain composure. The pain, which was nothing like the pressure of toes on scrotum, served to keep Peter focused. He maintained, every Tuesday, without an outburst. On those days that he did need to audition women, though, he made sure to spend a little extra time in the bathroom after the session, after lunch and after a coffee break, minimum, to "quell" those urges. The binder clip only did so much and, after a Tuesday casting session, nothing short of a tornado could stop Peter from bee-lining to that executive restroom and releasing all that pressure.

Peter designed new prosthetics for the Institute, improved on old models and, generally, made life worth living for people who had no other recourse. He spent his days dreaming of and, in all reality, attempting to improve upon the design of the foot and he was happy.

He still bore the weight of his obsession, though, and, more and more frequently he would be making trips to the executive restrooms for what he told anyone that questioned his well-being was a terrible case of diarrhea. What Peter did in that bathroom, three or four times daily, was to gratify himself using whatever he had absconded with from the lab. Photos, AutoCAD drawings, maybe even a complete pros-thetic foot that he could rub on himself and, using the toilet lid, try and step on his own scrotum with. Regardless of how much he tried to quit, he couldn't stop thinking about feet, his mother's toes, the pain and pleasure.

Peter kept it quiet, did his job and went about his day like any other employee. His managers, and the Institute administration, noticed he wasn't very sociable but that, they reasoned, was the price they must pay for genius.

In all reality, Peter loathed himself. He loathed every fiber of his being and, even though he was helping people, he knew that he could never, ever stop. He would be a freak forever. On lonely weekends, Peter would even contemplate suicide. Things were building to a head and Peter felt that his entire life was spiraling out of control. Sooner or later he would be found out.

Then he met Velma.

4 THIS LITTLE PIGGY HAD NONE

Velma was a beautiful girl. Generally, Peter didn't concern himself with features above the knee, but she was striking. Her hair the color of rich mahogany provided a contrast to the emerald green eyes. Her skin was alabaster, dotted with faint red freckles across the bridge of her nose. She was petite, Peter believed, but her condition made it difficult to judge height. When she rolled into the room, Peter expected to look up, see a new patient that needed a fitting, and carry on with his day as usual. Instead, today, he saw Velma.

He was struck with her beauty, first and foremost, and was bowled over with her shyness. She was in a wheelchair, of course, legged people usually don't come for a fitting. Peter smiled as the girl approached and she could only steal glances up at him. He knew, from experience, that she was self-conscious about her condition… he dealt with a similar issue every day.

"Hello," Peter said.

"Hi," Velma returned.

That was it. Peter checked her chart and scanned through her medical history quickly. Her name was Velma Sanders. She was a double amputee, losing both of her legs as a child to cancer, and had multiple complications being fitted for prosthetics. She had just turned twenty and, after years of being told that she would just 'grow out' of a pair of legs, she was finally able to convince her doctor that it may be time to try something new.

Peter closed the chart and looked at Velma. He saw the pain and the hurt in her eyes when she chose to bless him with a glance and he knew, just knew, that he had to make a difference in this young woman's life. It was up to him.

It didn't occur to Peter at that point, but thoughts of feet and shoes and self-gratification held no purchase in his mind. He was, for lack of a better term, smitten.

No one was more surprised than Peter when he said, "Say, it's almost noon, right? Can I buy you lunch before we start?"

Shocked, Velma looked up at the young engineer, who was handsome and well-groomed, for a full ten seconds before shying away. "Uhh, sure? I guess," she said.

"Do you have plans?" Peter asked.

Velma shook her head.

"Did you eat?"

Velma shook her head again.

"Oh, jeez, I'm sorry! My name is Peter Adelman and I'll be making sure your prosthetics are perfect." Peter blushed at that. He didn't mean to give so much away so quickly.

Velma looked up as Peter turned away. She smiled, genuinely, for the first time in who knew how long.

"Thanks," she said.

Smiling, Peter stood and gripped the handlebars of the wheelchair firmly. With a little grunt, he whisked Velma away and off to lunch in the Institute's cafeteria.

Lunch with Peter and Velma, to anyone else, would not seem very eventful. They spoke, briefly, about one another, but spent a majority of the time looking away and taking small bites out of their food. For each of them, though, this was a huge milestone. They were each other's first date and, as Peter wheeled Velma to the elevator and back to the lab, he said as much, attempting to hide it as a thinly-veiled joke.

Velma knew, and Peter knew that Velma knew. They had just crossed a threshold together and, as these things are wont to do, that caused their relationship to burgeon.

Back in the lab, Peter required Velma to sit on an examination table and he lifted her up and helped to right her. He couldn't help but notice how light she was and that she smelled like fresh rainwater. He smiled as he rolled her pant legs up to expose the stubs of her legs. The smile was forced on. Peter found this particular aspect of the job loathsome.

He understood that the prosthetics were helpful and that he was called to create them but the sight, and touch, of limbs without feet never failed to sicken him. It was as if all the beauty in a body had been removed and he was left to deal with the muck that was leftover, the debris of a human's essence. Peter was a craftsman, an artist, and he made these poor, unfortunate souls whole again. Without feet they were, and he felt horrible even thinking this, monstrosities. Tortured sideshow performers whose mangled exteriors reflected what could only be the painful and mangled interiors. Peter could usually hold his revulsion in check through the process of measurement, bone density tests and the usual physical attributes that he needed to record in order to, quite literally, save the souls of these unfortunates.

Velma was different, though. Oh, he found her stumps displeasing, of course, and his gag reflex threatened, but he only need look into her face, green eyes blazing and set in ivory, for that nauseous feeling to pass. He found, after a few attempts, that he didn't have an adverse reaction to touching her stumps, either. The scar tissue wove an interesting pattern, telling the story of a desperate surgery many years ago. He found Velma's lack of feet and leg no less pitiful than the rest, but he did not perceive her to be monstrous. It was a new feeling, foreign, but he liked it.

Velma, bolstered by the near-admission in the elevator, felt much more comfortable and told Peter about her early life as he worked. She had been diagnosed with primary bone cancer as a child and, in an attempt to stop the spread of her disease, she had both of her legs amputated. The femurs of both legs were filled with Osteosarcoma tumors, 95% of which were malignant, and Velma's parents were faced with a choice: Amputation to destroy the spread of the cancer or a very long, very expensive non-amputation treatment. This was a decision by her parents and, faced with mounting medical costs, chose the route that was the most economical and would still provide their daughter with a standard of life that was acceptable.

Velma did not think that they had made a poor decision, but longed to find out what the other treatment (radiation, incredibly expensive drugs and a gamble). Velma had the surgery at four years old and, for all intents and purposes, had no legs her entire life. Velma was aware, though, just how different she was. After the surgery, her parents were different. Even as a child, she felt they were colder, more distant. Her mother didn't engage in the same manner. She wasn't as warm and, even at four, Velma had the sense that her mother avoided looking at her. Velma's father made valiant attempts, but he still couldn't bring himself to regard Velma a full and complete daughter. She had felt as if she was half a person (or less) for her entire life.

Velma understood. She could see how difficult it would be to have a handicapped daughter and she didn't begrudge her parents anything. There was never enough money, or enough insurance, to actually get a good set of prosthetic limbs so Velma suffered through sores, abrasions and infections on and around her stumps while she tried to use different sets of hand-me-down prosthetics. Since starting college, she had been able to acquire student insurance and applied to the Institute's hardship program, which brought her to Peter.

During her story, Peter shook his head in disbelief at the atrocities this poor girl had endured and nodded in agreement while listening to just how callus parents could be. When Velma related her experiences with hand-me-down prosthetics, Peter stood and took her face in his hands.

Shocked, Velma could only stare up at Peter. This was turning into a very different type of examination.

"You have been so brave," Peter said to Velma.

"Thank you," she squeaked out.

"I vow, right here and right now, that you will never have to wear prosthetics from dead people ever again."

"OK."

Peter and Velma gazed into one another's eyes and, from that point forward, they knew that something special had happened. An electric connection had been established and neither of their lives would be the same.

Peter finished the examination and started his paperwork. Velma thanked him and, as she rolled toward the double glass doors, Peter felt a pang of loss. It was irrational and illogical, but he felt like a sappy greeting card and 'missed her already.'

Peter leapt up and rushed for the door, stopping Velma.

"Velma!"

She turned, shocked. "Yes?"

"Would you have dinner with me… tonight?"

Velma looked down at her stumps, the usual place her vision traveled when she was nervous. "Are you serious?"

Peter nodded. They had already joked about a first date, so the second date should be no big deal.

Without a word, Velma nodded.

Peter smiled, ear to ear. "I will be done here soon; may I pick you up at six?"

Velma nodded, again.

"At the address in your file?"

Another nod.

"Good!" With that, Peter walked Velma to the elevator, watched as she got in and stared at the floor light indicators above the doors as she descended.

For the first time, in a long time, Peter was happy.

5 THIS LITTLE PIGGY WENT WEE, WEE, WEE...

Peter worked slavishly, day and night. He wanted nothing more than to provide Velma with the perfect prosthetic. He wanted to make her whole and he was devoted to her, and she him. Peter and Velma connected on a deep level, deeper than most couples. Both of them were possessed with this terrible shame. Velma for her legs (or lack thereof) and Peter for his desires. Neither of them spoke about these shames, it was never apparent that they could actually verbalize the truth to one another. They remained connected, close and loving even if both of them were unaware of what really melded their lives together.

Yet, Peter still lusted after feet. He simply could not help it. Of course, he kept the symptoms of his fetish at bay while working, and would never speak of it to Velma, but he fought that fight on a daily basis. This resulted in Peter throwing himself into the work and designing, calibrating and fitting new feet and legs to needy patients.

The prosthetic feet did nothing for him, sexually, that is. He knew that they were unreal, cold, sterile... none of the things that made feet desirable. These were the tools of his trade, not of his desire, yet he quested. For Velma, he would create the perfect prosthetic and change both of their lives forever. He was already toying with pneumatic gears to 'arch' a foot and a small heating element to keep the prosthetic from feel cold and artificial.

He was getting there, but still couldn't shake the need to bury his nose in a co-worker's running shoe after she returned from a lunchtime jog, for example. Peter stopped himself from grabbing her gym bag and running from the office, but it was a close call. His only recourse was to go home that evening and punish himself.

The first time Velma and Peter had sex was… awkward. They had been dating for around three months and, in that time, they had been comfortable with one another's company. Comfortable to kiss and hold hands at a film, or to snuggle together and watch television would suffice for only so long. Velma broached the subject at breakfast.

"Peter?" she asked.

"Yes, darling," he answered.

"Do you think it would be all right if we… we… umm, I'm not sure how to say this."

"Just say it! Whatever it is, we'll work it out!"

"I want you to make love to me."

Peter stared at Velma, shocked. The thought of sex, with her, never crossed his mind. He knew, intellectually, that it would be possible but without feet. Without the proper equipment, he wasn't sure. Peter's mind raced, looking for a way out, when his mouth went into business for itself.

"I thought you would never ask," he said.

Velma's face lit up. She beamed from ear to ear.

They made plans to have sex that very evening.

The entire work day was spent in a fog. Peter was worried. He didn't know what sex with a woman was like, the event with the Major effectively stunting his sexual growth. He thought he knew what it should be like, masturbating as much as he did. After careful consideration, he was sure that his lack of experience would not be a big deal since Velma's sexual 'revolution' was as equally mired in self-loathing as his.

He had more practical concerns. Peter wasn't sure that he could actually perform, sexually, if there were no feet involved. Peter spent the day terrified of a flaccid penis and an inability to satisfy a young woman that he truly cared deeply for. Traumatized, he made the trek home after work in the same haze that permeated the work day.

Upon his arrival home, Peter entered to find his apartment adorned in candles. Velma had a key, of course, and could easily let herself in and out after Peter's landlord added the handicap ramp, bringing the building up to code. Peter's heart swelled, no one had ever done something like this, just for him, before. Thoughts of non-performance, erectile dysfunction, and soul-crushing shame were forgotten.

Until Velma rolled into the room.

She was as beautiful as always, her face beaming. She sat in her wheelchair, naked. Largish, firm breasts announced her arrival.

Peter took her in from head to, well, knee. This was the first living, naked and shorn vagina he had ever seen and, in all reality, he should have finished in his pants long before his gaze stopped at Velma's exposed nubs. He had grown used to them, from a clinical standpoint, but the budding erection in his pants stopped at the sight of the folded, stitched and scarred skin that covered the end of Velma's legs.

Velma couldn't see Peter's disappointment in the dim light and held out her arms, indicating that her boyfriend, her would-be lover, should whisk her off her chair and take her to bed.

Swallowing hard, Peter did just that. Forcing back the gag reflex that threatened to spill his lunch over Velma's naked torso, Peter lifted her easily and with strong, steady strides, took her to the bedroom. He nearly lost it one more time as he laid Velma down and the nub of her leg caressed his outer thigh, but Peter valiantly fought back his sickness.

He stood next to the bed as Velma lay on the bed. Neither of them were quite sure what they should be doing at this point.

Velma opened her legs, inviting Peter in but he remained motionless. She smiled, wagging a finger at Peter, and positioned herself to face him.

"I know what you want," she said.

She did not, of course, but Peter couldn't convey that.

Without asking, Velma deftly undid Peter's belt buckle, button and zipper and, before he could question how his virginal girlfriend was so adept at that, he nearly exploded in pleasure.

Velma took Peter into her mouth and he stiffened immediately. Despite the nubs, the lack of feet and the uneasiness Peter felt, he knew at that precise moment that, even repulsed, his body would react normally to stimuli.

Being the first time, Velma only had to work at him for less than a minute before he let loose. Velma pulled away quickly and allowed Peter to expel himself in the general direction of the bed as she held on, milking the young man's last few moments.

With her free hand, Velma wiped her mouth and looked up at Peter.

"Girl has to do something to stay popular in high school, right?"

Peter nodded, his mind literally blown. The post orgasm fog lifted after a moment and he came to a couple of realizations: 1) physically, from the knees down, Velma disgusted him and 2) he now knew that, with the right kind of nudge, he could perform under pressure. Peter decided right then and there that Velma, the love of his life 90% of the time, would be the perfect punishment for his depraved, freakish nature.

Peter turned to Velma, positioning her on the bed in a basic missionary-esque sexual position taking special care to move her away from the puddle he had created. Velma sat up and took his member in her hand, kneading and working to try and resurrect it for her turn. To Peter's delight, his penis responded accordingly.

"I do love you," he said to Velma, and meant it.

"I love you, too," she returned.

Taking a deep breath, Kevin reached down with both hands and grabbed the ends of Velma's stumps, running his hand over the soft, rope-like scar tissue. He gagged and nearly gave up, but Velma's work with her hands proved too good, too intoxicating.

As she guided him into her, Peter pushed her stumps up and back, causing her to fall backwards. She moaned, arched her back and closed her eyes through the entire event, loving each second turning into each minute that Peter pleasured her. Unaware that the entire time, her lover was on the verge vomiting into her belly button.

Peter fought the urge to run screaming from the room and continued to thrust in and out of Velma. They climaxed together, loudly. Peter dropped Velma's stumps and collapsed next to her on the bed. She turned and smiled at him and he smiled back. Neither of them spoke.

Peter had discovered a proper penance, one befitting the cruelty of his mother and the self-flagellating doctrine (not literally, but according to Betty Jo) of the Methodists. Peter Adelman could have all the sex he wanted, whenever he wanted, but he could never, ever enjoy it.

6 ALL THE WAY HOME

Peter and Velma lived happily together for the next year. She moved in and played the dutiful fiancée, after a relationship upgrade, and performed her almost-wifely duties zealously.

Peter continued to work, still in love with Velma, and continued to try and perfect the prosthetic that would change her life. Every model he had was imperfect, flawed to some degree. Any flaw, at all, could prove disastrous.

Peter and Velma continued to sleep with one another, as well. According to Velma, the sex was wonderful, frequent, and everything she hoped for. In public, or to Velma, Peter said the same thing. In all reality, he used sex with Velma as a punishment. If had a particularly bad day, for example, and actually shoved his nose in to the receptionist's gym shoe or snatched a sock from someone's bag for later, the guilt would nearly kill him.

He would come home on these days, which were growing more and more frequent, and have sex with Velma, using her stubs and scar tissue in ways that he would never even have dreamed of . Licking the nubs, specifically the small flaps of skin where he knees were to begin, was incredibly erotic for Velma. Peter would lower himself down and fellate the nubs for her. His punishment for indiscretions was quick, severe and disgusting.

It was a Tuesday that destroyed Peter's life. Foot modeling day had become easier and easier over the year. Especially since Peter realized that he could pay his penance at any time with Velma. Privately, he called his apologist sex, using the 'magic stubs.' On that particular Tuesday, though, not even 'magic stubs' would be able to save Peter from himself, from his predilection or from Andrea.

Andrea Martin was the last model of the day for Peter and his team. In all reality, most foot models or volunteers are unfit for prosthetic molding or further investigation of the mechanics of the foot. Peter and the others would look, take some photos, take some notes, mark the chart and politely send the model on his or her way.

Not today.

Andrea entered the room and kicked off a pair of heels like a pro. She walked lightly, lithely on the balls of her feet and pranced in front of the judges.

Peter took one look at Andrea's feet and knew, in his heart, that he was about to ruin his own life. Peter didn't even bother to look past Andrea's ankles. Standing before him were a pair of the most perfect feet he had ever seen. Peter had studied for years, looking for a foot that as not only aesthetically pleasing, including an arch that rose approximately ½ inch above the floor. He could tell they were a size 6, equally, without any toenail polish, rings or tattoos to mar the rightness of it all.

Andrea's toes were in a 45 degree formation combing down, from largest to smallest, after the perpendicular right angle created by the big toe and line of five, exquisite toe joints.

Both right and left were perfectly symmetrical.

Andrea's flesh was a light olive and Peter could see that she took fine care of her feet. He could see the tell-tale markings (to him) of a pumice stone, daily manual callus removal, and frequent moisturizing. He skin was nearly reflective.

After gaping at Andrea's feet, Peter finally managed to scan her file, finding out that a woman named Andrea Martin stood before him and not a disembodied pair of feet. He looked up to see that the rest of Andrea's body was stunningly beautiful, too. Peter shook his head, trying to clear it. This had to be some kind of daydream or hallucination. He had just stumbled upon Mecca, paradise… everything.

"Peter," the other designer in the room said. "Are you all right?"

Peter grinned and nodded. He looked up at Andrea again, this time actually looking at her face and into her eyes.

She grinned as if she knew exactly what was going through his mind. She nodded and held her hand out.

Peter stood, took her hand, and walked her back to her shoes. He was lost. All was lost. If he passed this up he wouldn't be able to live with himself. Sadly, it took less than thirty seconds for Peter to throw his entire life away. There was no amount of amputee-sex with Velma that could take the thought of Andrea's feet away.

"I'm afraid I must worship you," Peter told the young woman. He noticed that she was a brunette, finally, and quite stunning.

"I'm thought as much," she said. "Follow me." Andrea stooped, picked up her heels, and handed them to Peter. Without skipping a beat, he shoved his face as far into the toe of the shoe as he could and sniffed.

Peter's fellow designer, Lenny, and the division assistant in the room could do nothing but stare at their colleague. Peter Adelman, as far as they knew, was the most conservative, straightest, most dedicated engineer that had ever passed through those doors. He was getting married to a double amputee, for Christ's sake, and was working on giving her a pair of beautiful, perfect legs as a wedding present. Or, that was until Andrea Martin auditioned.

Peter turned to his fellow staffers, reluctantly pulled the shoe away from his face, and resigned.

"I resign, effective immediately," Peter said and turned for the door.

"Peter, wait! What about Velma?" Lenny asked.

Peter stopped for a moment, just a moment. He turned and, without batting an eye, said, "Would you mind calling her and telling her that I have to leave? Andrea is here."

With that, Peter shoved his face back into the toe of the high heel and followed Andrea Martin, and her perfect feet, from the building.

7 HAPPILY EVER AFTER

Peter didn't really think of Velma anymore. When he followed Andrea from the building and to her small condo downtown, he didn't really require much more than that. As far as he knew, Velma had gone through much worse in her life. She was strong and could take care of herself. He was also sure that someone at the Institute, like Lenny, would take over his designs and make sure that she was going to be all right as far as the prosthetic was concerned. Anyway, he had more important things to deal with.

Andrea, on a personal level, remained a mystery to Peter. He lived there, in her condo. He wasn't sure what she did for a living, if anything, or if she had some sort of trust fund. Regardless, she was his mistress and he worshipped her feet. Simple formula. She would feed him from time to time, because he would forget to eat, and she would tell him to bathe, because he would forget to clean himself regularly.

What he did not forget to do was to caress, massage, taste, clean, and devote himself to Andrea's feet on a daily basis. He woke thinking of that perfect pair and went to sleep satisfied in his appreciation of them only to dream of those gorgeous, symmetrical beauties until he would wake and repeat the process.

Andrea would jog every morning and, after removing her socks and shoes, Peter would collect them up and dart to the small walk-in closet where he lived. Andrea had made a bed for him there on the first evening and he nested ever since, pulling pieces of footwear (Andrea's) around him to form a makeshift bed.

While in his little area, with the sweat socks and shoes, Peter would make a daily ritual of rubbing Andrea's socks all over his body, keeping that scent, eventually ejaculating into one of the socks. He would then smell her shoes until he was called for.

Anyone who could see Peter now, less than a month removed from his position at the Institute and his caring, if dysfunctional, relationship with Velma, would be shocked. He was much thinner and had the look of a beaten dog, wanting desperately to please his superiors but afraid of what would be withheld or denied at any moment. Peter's transformation was so complete, and so sudden, it may have surprised Andrea, even.

While living in the condo, Peter could see the evidence of past co-habitants. A pair of pants in the closet, or a studded collar that he knew had been used at one point (just not by him). Andrea would even mention past 'worshippers,' as she called them, but always made sure she let Peter know how special he was and how much she appreciated him. Deep, deep down, Peter knew that Andrea had done this before. She knew where to find men like him and she walked in, literally, and left with them in tow like some kind of perfect-footed Pied Piper. She knew she would find Peter, or someone like Peter, at the Institute. Someone that, when faced with her below-ankle assets, could no longer deny their own desires.

To Peter, Andrea seemed ageless. She wasn't old, but she wasn't young. She was, for all intents and purposes, perfect and he never intended to leave. Briefly, at one point, he was curious as to the fate of her other worshippers but he could only surmise that she grew tired of them. This panicked Peter and he pushed it out of his mind by vowing to never cease, to never ease up in his devotion to Andrea. He would do anything for her. Anything, and that let Peter sleep at night, surrounded by his mistresses' old shoes.

Andrea, of course, was well aware of the effect her assets had on a podophiliac mind. She took great care to maintain her feet, as Peter noticed upon their first meeting. That included toe hair electrolysis, non-chemical pedicures, moisturizing baths, etc., etc. She was a trust fund baby, living off the assets of being the heiress to the owners of the bakery that made cookies shaped like garden gnomes. Lucrative, if boring.

Andrea searched out men like Peter in exactly the manner she found him. They seemed to gravitate toward prosthetics, oddly enough, and their kind was the only kind she had found to date that could devote themselves so fully to her that she could take care of a dark little secret of her own.

Andrea called Peter out from his nest one day, making sure he had finished with the sweat sock and before he began the ritual cleaning. He scampered from the room and sat at her feet, cross-legged on the floor while Andrea stood.

"Are you happy, Peter?"

"Very much so!"

Andrea squinted at Peter, displeased.

"I'm sorry! Very much so, mistress!" Peter said.

Andrea smiled, "Much better. I'm glad that you're happy. But, I must admit, I'm not."

Peter's entire countenance changed. His shoulders slumped and he looked up at Andrea on the verge of tears. "Why are you unhappy?"

Andrea smiled down at him, pleased that her unhappiness caused him so much pain. "I need something more, Peter. I need to feel excited… like you. I excite you, don't I?"

Peter nodded his head, a smile springing to his lips.

"You enjoy my feet, don't you, Peter?"

Peter nodded again, instinctively gazing down at them. He moaned a little, they were so close.

"I have something that makes me feel like that, too," Andrea said. "But it is something that not everyone can do."

Peter looked up. He wanted more than anything to please Andrea. To date, he had yet to see her naked or even attempt gratify herself. It did make him feel a bit selfish, but he couldn't help it. "What can I do to help? I'll do anything, I promise!"

Andrea smiled but shook her head. "I can't ask you to do that. It is too much. My pleasure isn't important." She sighed there, long and protracted.

Peter nearly fell apart watching her melancholy display. "Please, mistress, Andrea, let me do this for you!"

Andrea looked up, wiping away non-existent tears and smiled. She held her hand out and Peter took it. She pulled him to his feet and let him toward her bedroom. They entered and walked back toward the large closet (much larger than the guest room closet Peter slept in) and opened the door. He had never been in here.

As the doors opened, Peter thought he had died and entered heaven. Rows upon rows of shoes stared back at him. Andrea possessed all types. From formal to informal, flip flops to knee-high studded boots, it appeared as if one of everything had a place in this room.

Andrea pulled Peter farther into the closet that felt like it went on forever until they reached a small door in the rear. She turned to him.

"Peter, very few people know about this room. I'm trusting you with a great deal, here."

Peter nodded, barely able to pull his eyes away from shoe Mecca.

Andrea opened the door and they both entered. She pulled on a chain from the ceiling and a dim, 100 watt bulb sprang to life revealing a dentist's chair. The room had a small cabinet on one side, the dentist's chair and the light bulb. The walls and floor were gray concrete and unadorned.

Peter looked to Andrea, unsure of what was happening. "Andrea? What is…"

"Excuse me?" she asked.

"I'm sorry. *Mistress*, what are we doing in here?"

Andrea frowned, conjuring up the crocodile tears once again. "I thought you wanted me to feel as good as you do, Peter. I thought it was the fair thing…"

Peter nodded, smiling. "You're right. You're right. It's fair. What should I do?"

Recovering quickly, Andrea pointed to the dentist's chair. "Sit down."

Peter obeyed instantly and swung into the chair. He looked at Andrea, smiling.

Without another word, she walked around the chair, strapping Peter in with leather restraints. First at his wrists, then his feet and, finally, his head. She tugged each of them to make sure that they were secure and then spun Peter in the chair to face her.

"Peter, I have a small confession to make. I am an acroto-mophiliac. I know this is something that you aren't familiar with. I also know that when something like this happens, it overtakes you... you can't help how you feel. There is no control. Am I right?"

Peter attempted to nod, but the leather strap prevented it. "Yes," he said.

"Good. I need you to do something for me. So I can have some satisfaction, too."

"Okay. What is an acromo... phila...?"

"I am sexually attracted to, and wish to pleasure myself, with amputees. It is acrotomophilia."

Peter's eyes grew wide, "But I'm not..."

Andrea looked down at Peter and smiled, stroking his hair. "No, no you're not and that is why I've asked you here. What I have, this thing that controls me, is too far gone. Regular amputees just don't cut it anymore. In order for this to happen, I need your help. I need to take a finger here, or a toe there, Peter. Give those to me and make me feel as good as you do. Please?"

Peter took a moment for the information to register. She was asking him to lose a finger or a toe or a hand? He couldn't shake his head to clear it, but was pretty confident that Andrea meant what she said. Peter grunted, ready to ask Andrea to give him more time. He had made the decision to leave his job, Velma and the world instantly, but this was a little different.

Andrea had a different plan. Balancing on one leg she raised her other leg in the air. Lithe, like a dancer, she placed her naked foot on Peter's lower lip.

His resolve shook.

Andrea flipped Peter's lip with her perfectly perpendicular big toe and traced a trail down Peter's chest with her foot. She made it to his abdomen.

Any slack in Peter's pants was taken up quickly as every ounce of blood in his body rushed to his crotch.

Andrea ran her foot down the length of Peter's trapped erection and finally landed on his scrotum. She applied a little pressure, grabbing and releasing Peter's balls with her toes through the pants.

He moaned; the pain was exquisite.

"Peter, may I take a finger?" Andrea asked.

Peter moaned again as she applied slightly more pressure to his scrotum. "Just a finger?" he asked.

"Just a finger," Andrea said as she pushed into Peter's gonads. His breath caught in his throat, so extreme was the pleasure and the jabbing pain running through his lower abdomen.

After a moment, Peter moaned loudly, breathing out a long "Yeeessss," as his pants grew darker and moister.

Andrea pulled her foot down from the chair and looked up at Peter. She smiled.

"How did you know about…?"

"You talk about your mother in your sleep, silly. It was the least I could do. I'll get the scalpel."

ANDREA USED AN ANESTHETIC, KNOCKING PETER OUT with a gas mixture before she began. He sucked in the happy fumes through a mask and, before he knew it, Peter was out.

She did confide in him a few things prior to the surgery. She was a residency away from a medical degree. Andrea was put on an administrative leave due to inappropriate sexual conduct with a patient. The patient was a war veteran, missing a hand, and he was more than happy to help Andrea out with her issue, but a nurse had come in to see the young would-be-doctor riding the patient's stump and that was enough to end Andrea's medical career. She just wanted Peter to know that she was trained and that nothing would go wrong.

Peter came to approximately an hour later to feel his arm being manipulated. He looked down, still hazy from the surgery, to find his arm missing at the elbow. If this wasn't shocking enough, he felt his arm wiggling because it was. Andrea had climbed aboard the dentist's chair, straddled Peter's prone body, and rubbed clitoris violently with the stitched and sutured stub.

Peter tried to scream only to find that he had been gagged.

Andrea was very near the end when Peter woke and came, quite loudly, letting what remained of his arm drop to the side. After she opened her eyes, all post-orgasmic quaking subsided, Andrea smiled.

"Sorry about that, Peter. I get a little carried away sometimes." With that, she hopped down from the dentist's chair, shut off the light and closed the door as she left Peter in the darkness.

8 THE END

It would happen like that, day after day. Andrea would knock Peter out, take a little more and then pleasure herself with either whatever remained, whatever was taken or both. Peter was put under so much anesthesia that he couldn't be sure what was real or what wasn't real. All he knew is that prior to every surgery, Andrea squished, squeezed, and stepped on his testicles to the point he could barely stand it anymore and, no matter how hard he tried to fight it, his body responded in the same way every time.

The remainder of his arm. A foot. Then up to the knee. Then the hip. Start over on the other side at the hand again. Little by little, pieces of Peter Adelman disappeared and, for his sacrifices, he lived out the fantasy that began with is mother over and over again.

But all good things must come to an end.

Peter woke after the last surgery thinking that the last bit of his last leg would be gone (he couldn't see that far down with the leather strap on his head) and planned on staring at that single, naked light bulb above his head until Andrea finished herself off. This was different, though. For starters, he could open his mouth and make a sound.

He looked around the area to find the room was brightly lit, with white walls. It smelled good, too, like peppermint. He raised his head, blinking against the light, and made out two shapes in front of him. They were in white shirts, or coats, or something similar. He would need to wait until his vision cleared.

Vocal cords, unused in a week, rattled, "Excuse me."

The white coats turned quickly and stepped closer. Peter could see that they were medical types. Doctors. Doctors? That means hospital. Peter smiled. He was away. She gave him away!

"Hello, sir. My name is Dr. Draven," the first white blob said. "I don't want you to panic. We are doing the best we can here."

"Where is she?" Peter managed to get out.

"Where is who?" Dr. Draven asked.

"Andrea. She brought me here. Let me... go."

"I'm sorry, sir, you were found propped up outside in the snow. Wait just a minute and we'll get you some water."

Doctor Draven turned and left the room, followed by the other white blob. Peter could feel where his arms and legs used to be, but he knew they weren't there anymore. Andrea, if that was her real name, had taken what she needed and discarded the rest. If this had happened to another person, Peter may have even seen the irony in it. Not this time. Now he knew what had happened to her other worshippers. They stopped being useful.

Peter laid his head back on the pillow and shut his eyes. He heard someone enter the room humming to herself and, despite everything that had happened, he wondered if she was wearing sensible, white nurse's shoes.

PUNK ROCK!

THE COPROPHAGUS

He had, quite literally, saved the world time and again. He was not the bringer of light. He was the dweller of darkness. He did not forgive and bless and hold the world to his bosom. He was the dark star. The swirling miasma of the universe's piss and vinegar given unto man as a living and breathing mortal latrine and heavy bag, coming only once a millennia to clean the sins of the planet. Reviled, misunderstood and persecuted, he was still absolutely necessary, and when his time on this planet passed, we had to wait... are still waiting... for another of his kind to emerge.

Every welt and bruise on his mortal body shifted the people of the world into the light. He took the punishment that humanity so desperately deserved. He consumed the blackest deeds, forcing them down his throat and allowing the undeserving citizens of the planet absolution. These deeds, these sins, came to him as filth. Piles of steaming, rancid waste matter. Feces and urine. Piss and shit. Vomit and semen and blood. All of it. Every horrible act that every horrible human could devise manifested itself as pain or bodily matter and the savior's task was to shoulder the burden. Eat the pain. Eat the shit. Eat the sin. He was the Sin-Eater.

Like other Sin-Eaters before him, he neither wanted the job nor enjoyed it. The balance of the cosmos was on the line though, and fate dealt him the same hand it had dealt countless other sentient beings over the eons. And, much like those other beings, the people he saved, the members of his species that benefitted from the pain and misery, looked upon him as a pariah. They hated him or, as some have suggested, hated the idea that he had to exist.

This one in particular was reviled by his own people more than most, but for a very good reason… he made them face their crimes. The abuse that wracked his mortal frame was put on display. Each dripping handful of sin he crammed down his own throat was committed to posterity via late twentieth century technology. If he had to suffer, then they would learn the price of their sins. For the universe gave unto man a thoroughly forgotten son to take their pain and misery onto and into his own self. Born Jesus Christ Allin, he was the Sin-Eater. He was the Coprophagus.

I am Demeter and I have been tasked with telling the story of the Coprophagus' last battle. The one that eventually consumed *him*. As a neophyte in a forgotten order, I am not important, but this record must be made available to the next Sin-Eater and the next. The next Avatar of Putrescence must know of his legacy, that of Allin, greatest among them.

Chosen at birth to shoulder the burden, he spent years under the guise of a musician, showing the young people of the planet what it was he had to do for them. Many misunderstood. Many took the grandiose acts as nothing more than an attempt to shock and destroy the traditional American values they so hotly defended. In the great irony of the Coprophagus, those values were exactly what he had to consume, night after night. The atrocities committed in the name of real Americans pummeled his body from head to foot, breaking bones, tearing skin and rending flesh. Unlike other Sin-Eaters, he gave voice to it.

"Stick me down, step on my face, spit on me. 'Cause I don't scare, you'll see. Make me bleed," he would scream to them from the stage. The young people would dance and punch and kick and cut and slice and stab and he cared not. Every one of them inadvertently provided solace unto the world. Each puncture wound bleeding from the top of Allin's head, mixing with the sweat and tears as it flowed down his chest and onto the stage, edged the world closer into karmic balance. "Gonna do what I want. Fuck you. I don't care what you do to me. Make me bleed."

Analogous to other so-called saviors, whose tiny faiths are measured merely in years and not the age of the cosmos, the Coprophagus would call them to him. All their anger, all their hate and all their violence coalesced, and he allowed them to vent those frustrations on his literal body. Of his flesh. Of his blood. The young people who saw nothing but a bleak future, squandered by their forefathers, took the literal pound of flesh from the Sin-Eater and, without even knowing it, their futures brightened. He would call to them, a singsong of recognition. "Some fuckhead in the corner's getting to me. Talkin' about the way I look and smell. Well I guess he don't know that I'm the Outlaw Scumfuc. Someone oughta warn him before I knock him straight to Hell."

Humans are despicable though, and, no matter the threshold of pain even the greatest among Coprophagus could endure, the year nineteen hundred and ninety three, by the Roman calendar, proved too much even for Allin. Vile act after vile act, plunging the world itself into a deeper and deeper pit, threatened to overtake the light and forever tip the balance in favor of Chaos. For it is the Lords of Chaos, who existed when the stars were young, that drive corporeal forms into maelstroms. Their need to remake existence in any random image drives them. The Lords of Order have not been heard from since the birth of the planets, yet their Avatar, the Sin-Eater, remains to struggle against the breach. In that year, the year we lost the Sin-Eater, he consumed chaos itself and gave humanity a chance.

As humans are wont to do, and American humans in particular, acts of violence, rage, intolerance, hate, torture, murder, rape, etc. are fairly common. These were the normal sins that the Coprophagus would abolish from the planet. They would build in intensity, from small flesh wounds and bruises and welts covering a multitude of transgressions, to large-scale events akin to genocide and war that required the Sin-Eater to consume the shit and piss and vomit. He needed to make the world whole and that was what he did.

In March of 1992, the Sin-Eater visited the den of the trickster. A media manipulator who sought to turn the public against its own self-interest. The being called "Geraldo" by some was just another agent of chaos. Allin fought valiantly, preserving the truth. He needed to be. He had to be. Without a "him," without a Sin-Eater, they would all be lost because only in that comparison could man feel right about himself. The species knew, even if they refused to admit it, that they were a cowardly, violent lot and had to feel superior to something. The Geraldo only helped to further that cause, which was the price one paid for dealing in chaos… it rarely went as planned. Even in vanquishing the beast, the Sin-Eater was weakened and unprepared for the monumental trials ahead.

January of 1993, the Sri Lanka Navy executed one hundred civilians for no apparent reason. This came on the heels of the dissolution of Czechoslovakia, which brought its own brand of Eastern European barbarism into the world.

Fresh off the battle with the puppet of the Lords of Chaos, the Sin-Eater shoveled steaming piles of his own, and others, fecal matter into his mouth. He gagged as it caked his teeth and gums. He could only breathe through his nose and that dried the filth around his lips, causing them to crack and splinter when he cried out, suffering. These sins were heavy.

In February, James Bolger, a cute ten-year-old boy, was abducted, tortured, sexually assaulted, and murdered by two other boys. This was the appetizer. A bomb at New York's World Trade Center exploded, killing six and injuring over 1000. His body wracked with pain, taking abuse night after night to wash these hateful, spiteful acts away, the Coprophagus bent backwards and accepted hot, acidic washes of vomit leaving the throats of innumerable donors. Later that month, the United States government raided David Koresh and the Branch Davidian compound. As the Sin-Eater knew, the individual, no matter how depraved, could never hold a candle to what the duly elected or installed or assigned governments of nations could do. That act began a 51 day siege.

The Coprophagus continued balancing the world. His head, split asunder time and again, washed his near naked body in blood, and yet he continued on, despite the pain. He could not ignore it, no being could, but he relished it. The box cutter across the forearm filleted the tissue and muscle, rending the flesh to the bone, gleaming white under the stage lights. The audience cheered... they could not fathom why but they needed this. Their world depended on it. He whispered to them, cooing, "Laying on the floor in a pool of blood and cum. My demons lay beside as I kiss them one by one. Then on that day I met a force that nothing will compare. I was born the son of evil when I fuck the devil there."

March bled into April. Nuclear accidents in Russia, the

war in Bosnia raged amid calls of human rights violations, and on the 19th of the month, the Branch Davidians failed to hold against their oppressors. Seventy-six men, women, and children were consumed in fire for the sake of their religion, and Chaos chuckled.

The Sin-Eater consumed and consumed and consumed. Hot urine, burning the cuts and welts on his face, streamed over Allin's form as he filled himself with even more shit and piss. The stage was littered with filth as the Coprophagus used the bile of a fan as lubricant and he slipped the large, unwieldy microphone in his rectum. The soft, sensitive skin ripped and bled as the acidic bile stung the open wounds. Yet he needed to press on. Man's inhumanity knew no bounds and he had to be boundless, too. As it ripped and tore and burned, he cried to the heavens, "Pulled out my burning pecker and out came the puss. Though it hurt, but I was devoured by lust. Oh, what a fuck."

May and June rushed toward the Sin-Eater. Reeling from the fire that ate women and children alive, the Bosnian conflagration continued. Lorena Bobbitt sliced her husband's penis off and the Unabomber continued his reign of mail order terror. Pakistani soldiers were massacred in Somalia and IRA bombs destroyed innocent bus riders on the Emerald Isle. Finally, the new President of the United States ordered missiles to be launched in Iraq in retaliation for the assassination plot on his predecessor. The cycle continued.

The Coprophagus took it all in, literally and figuratively. Under the guise of "punk rock," his valiant battle against the Lords of Chaos and their minions raged. His body wracked with abrasions and cuts and tumors and lumps, the Sin-Eater could barely move as he ate sin after sin. The shit of the world filled the gaps in his teeth. Yellow diarrhea caked his mustache.

Barely able to move, let alone actively ingest sins, Allin

laid on his back and willed himself to vomit upward. A stomach full of partially digested blood and cum, piss and shit expelled into the air. He closed his eyes as the stomach acid and its contents rained down. He opened his mouth, hoping against hope that this would set the world right, that this act of vileness could redeem the world enough to set the balance straight again.

And it did.

The resiliency of the Coprophagus' human form had reached a limit, but the world reset in that act. Disease filled him. Pestilence embraced him. That last, brilliant act had saved the world one last time. Allin's mortal coil, slipping from his grasp, was only temporary anyway. Like any savior, he knew his time in this existence had a limit. Smiling, the Sin-Eater consumed one last thing and, when he was done, he lay back and waited to stop breathing.

Right before he met the Lords of Order and left the world, there is a story among believers that he eulogized the struggle and sacrifice. On June 28th, barely audible, the Sin-Eater, the Coprophagus, the Avatar of Putrescence, whispered, "Now I'm ready to close my eyes. And now I'm ready to close my mind. And now I'm ready to feel your hand. I'm gonna fuck you now in the burning sands."

I am Demeter and we await the next Sin-Eater. He or she is sorely missed. The years since the time of Allin have proven difficult. The Lords of Chaos have simply waited and allowed the worst in humanity to flourish. There is no balance. There is no one to consume our sins. They are out and open. The world suffers. We suffer.

Still, we wait.

SPACE OPERA!

HAZMAT

CHAPTER ONE

L eon Rizzowski hated, hated, hated his job. As a geneticist in school, he had envisioned a life of research, grants, pretty young coeds as interns, and a life of relative luxury. He would teach a class here or there, and a teaching assistant would handle the grading. He was good enough to keep school and corporate administrations interested in his work and could present with the best of them—there would be no end of money. Except for this one, lousy decision.

The twenty-five-year-old researcher turned from the large screen before him. He had been monitoring the cellular division of an organism that the company was interested in developing that could, potentially, serve as a living exo-suit enabling a human being to withstand the rigors of space in, essentially, a living space suit, oxygenating the individual as they repaired spacecraft, marched across alien terrain, or did orbital research. There were many applications. Each of them bored Rizzowski to death, and against protocol, he looked away.

Leon was 'blessed' with a small portal in his lab. He, like the other thirty researchers on the project, had their own lab. They would meet for meals and what passed for recreation and rest in the bunker area. The complex itself was interesting, Rizzowski had to give the developers that. A central, large bunker area was the housing complex. Thirty researchers and thirty support staff. Like spokes on a wheel, long hallways shot out into the each of the individual thirty labs. Leon had an idea what was going on in each of them; they were briefed. He was the geneticist, and it was his task to refine the 'material,' the living matter that would form the basis of the suit. He didn't pay attention to much else, giving the rest of the staff the idea that he was aloof. He wasn't, he was apathetic. He did notice Dr. Andrea Kusick, though. Her task was in bio-mechanical engineering—i.e., making the organism work with and respond to the mechanics of the exo-suit. Rizzowski smiled thinking about her. He was sure that she was quite intelligent and deserved to be there, but all he could think about was her body. Her magnificent body. Seven months on this ice cube, and he was getting tired of the five finger tango.

Which brought him back to the portal. Each lab had a large window (made from the same polymer that star craft windshields are made of) that looked out upon the ... unique landscape. In order to keep the project quiet, the corporation had decided that a remote locale would be best. They chose Cenaturi Six. This was the smallest and most remote planet in the Centauri System ,and therefore, looked to be nothing more than one large ice ball spinning in the farthest orbit from its nearest star.

Rizzowski looked out at that inhospitable and frigid landscape and sighed. The structure itself was warm and provided whatever a human could need, but the planet was nothing more than rocks and jagged ice. It stretched out as far as Leon could see in the dim light provided by the distant star. Routinely, the planet would dip to -78 degrees Celsius. The planet was thought to be uninhabited and the entirety of the staff could not think of any organism that humanity had yet to run into in the past 700 years of space exploration that could survive Centauri Six.

Leon sneered. That was the other reason. He figured that this frozen rock in the middle of absolute nowhere that included a zero chance of outdoor survival beyond fifteen seconds or so would be the perfect place to create a new organism that could withstand the rigors of space — and keep it at bay if things went wrong.

Continuing to ignore the screen in front of him, Rizzowski stared out at the ice rock. He absentmindedly lifted a coffee mug to take a sip, forgetting that it was stone cold. He realized too late and choked down the sip of frozen coffee and stood up. He glanced at the monitor briefly to see that there was another twenty minutes left in the cellular division cycle and stood up. The ice cold coffee was enough excuse to see what Dr. Kusick was up to and take another shot at getting her to open up … in more ways than one.

Leon gave the landscape through the portal the finger and whistled as he began the hike down the spoke hallway to his lab, to the common room for some coffee, and off to see Dr. Kusick.

What he didn't notice was the small, flashing light on the monitor. Had Leon been paying attention, he would have seen that the cellular division had picked up pace. Strictly monitored, the organisms would only be allowed to grow so large for testing, and through the history of the project, these organisms had divided and expanded at a well-regulated rate. Of course, he had considered the concept that the biomaterial could expand beyond the defined rates that had been established, but like everything else here, that would be far too exciting.

The flashing red light grew as the organism grew. When the division hit a certain point, a bunker-wide alarm sounded. The shrill, clarion call echoed down the spokes, in the common areas, and in the labs. In the middle of the spoke to the central area, Leon Rizzowski slowly turned and stared at his lab. The coffee mug fell from his hand and shattered on the ground. He knew.

Rizzowski sprinted toward the lab as fast as he could. From the training manuals, he knew that the five-person security detail response time was around four minutes. If what was happening was what he thought it was, he didn't know if that four minutes would be enough. For the project-wide alarm to kick in, things had to have gotten out of control quickly.

As Leon Rizzowski, PhD found out as he entered the lab, that was the understatement of, quite possibly, all scientific study from Galileo and forward.

CHAPTER TWO

Dr. Andrea Kusick—Andi to her friends who seemed so far away from Centauri VI— jumped in her chair as the alarm echoed throughout the complex. Their training had included protocols for this particular alarm, and those protocols included shutting down her work lab immediately.

Andrea leapt from her console where she had just finished putting together what she thought could be the synaptic response leads that could combine the organism to the mechanical structural source that would not only give it form, but allow the mechanics to 'talk' to the organism and vice versa. That geneticist, Leon Rizzowski, insisted on calling it a 'smart suit.' very time he did, it grated on Andrea's nerves. She wasn't sure if it was the name or the fact that it was coming out of Rizzowski's mouth. She loathed the man and had him pegged as a misogynistic lowlife the minute she laid eyes on him. That, of course, didn't stop his little visits. She wondered from time to time if he visited any of the other researchers with his special brand of wit. It was impressive, though, the amount of rejection the man could take.

Regardless, Andrea dove into action. When the alarm went off, they were trained to shut down their projects and back up the information to the site server. Once the data was collected, it would be transmitted securely to the main office on Earth. She was then to meet her fellow scientists in the bunker area and get further instructions. Andrea started the information relay, and just to be safe, packed the synaptic relays. They were useless, of course, without the mechanical components of the 'smart suit' in another lab, but she liked to be thorough.

Andrea turned, ready to head to the bunker, when she was greeted with exactly what she thought she might find in an emergency: Leon Rizzowski's libido. Standing before her was the geneticist. He leaned against a lab table, leering at her. He grinned.

"Dr. Kusick. Hello there."

Andrea glared at the man as she hefted the case with the relays in it.

"Leon, are you serious? We have an emergency. Get to the lab, and take care of your part of the project."

Leon smiled again. "Taken care of."

Shaking her head, Andrea moved to push past the young doctor. Her hand moved toward his arm, but she ran into something unexpected. At least a full inch before she touched his arm Andrea's fingers sank into an opaque, gelatinous substance. It had the consistency of a stiff gelatin and appeared to surround Rizzowski's body. She stepped back, shocked.

"Leon? Is that... the... the..."

Rizzowski smiled. He stepped forward and faltered a bit, catching himself on the table.

Andrea could see the gelatinous skin fall down, exposing Leon's face for a moment. The moment his face was exposed, Leon gasped for air. His eyes grew panicked, and he shouted at the terrified young woman in front of him.

"Andrea! The organism needs the relays... the suit... stop it. Can't hold all the time. Make sure..."

Before Rizzowski could finish, the organism covered him one more time. The leer returned. The panicked look on the scientist's face disappeared.

"Leon?"

"Give or take. Give me the relays, Andrea." The Leon-thing stepped forward. It sounded as if he were walking through a swampy marsh, each step punctuated by an organic squish.

Andrea backed up. "Even if you get these, you don't have the rest of the project."

"We will, soon." Leon advanced.

Andrea knew that the organism was unstable without a structure; it couldn't hold Leon indefinitely, but she couldn't count on it happening again. Andrea took a deep breath and prepared run past and through Leon if she had to.

As she moved forward, Leon's hand shot towards her. The organism stretched from Leon's fingertips and toward the young scientist. It wrapped around her head and chest, squeezing and groping as it flowed around her. Andrea struggled for a moment, fighting against the amorphous substance as it surrounded her, flowed into her nose and mouth. She gagged as the stuff oxygenated her, and Andi Kusick learned to breath in a whole new manner. She relaxed. The organism didn't speak to her, per se, but it communicated. She was part of it. Her and Leon.

It took a moment for Andi and Leon to get of shed their clothes. The organism pulsed in and round them, embracing them without the hindrance of human apparel they would no longer need. Direct contact, organism to human skin, made the bond stronger, but it still wasn't complete.

Andrea scooped up the relay case, and hand in hand, she and Leon grinned as they moved toward the bunker and the remaining project leaders. If there was an emergency, then they were to meet and receive further instructions.

CHAPTER THREE

Colonel Andrew Gage received the communication from the client nearly thirty minutes ago. In that time, he assessed the situation and called together the team. A former military specialist, Gage had been in the private sector for the past ten years working in the janitorial field, as his ex-wife called it. For the first few years, he grated his teeth every time she said it. He gave up, eventually, and embraced the term. He was an intergalactic janitor. The best out there as a matter of fact. When the bitch allowed him to talk to his daughter Rylene, the eight-year-old would start every conversation with following question: *Hey, daddy, how do you clean up the universe?* Gage would respond in the same way every time: *With a very big broom.* He hadn't been able to have that conversation as often as he would have liked lately and made a mental note to rectify that situation right after this job.

This job. He sighed. He looked over the specs again as he waited for the rest of the team. Centauri VI. Great. Ex-wife frigid with a zero percent survival rate if the team misses their extraction. Much more than a janitor, of course, Andrew Gage led the best Hazmat team in four star systems.

Chemical, biological, or irradiated materials… or just about anything that the client deemed to be 'hazardous' fell under the auspices of the team. He had taken care of pre-melt-down 20th century nuclear warheads on Earth all the way to carnivorous bacteria the size of a small child and most everything in-between. He was used to dealing with the worst problems and making sure that the scenario was a win-win—at least for his team and the client. What he looked at on the briefing sheet was something new, though. It didn't worry him, he loved the challenge, but he was surprised at how little the client knew about their own lab and the work going on there. It smelled governmental, and Gage learned a long time ago to trust his nose. He was a janitor, after all.

Centauri VI Lab was designed to house thirty separate components of a project using organic material to create a mechanized survival suit that could endure deep space. Biological aspects, mechanical aspects, faulty firmware and software aspects, and an unknown power source that could be comprised to make the suit function.

Gage whistled. This had a little bit of everything.

"What's up, Colonel?"

Gage lifted his head. Before him, assembled and ready to move exactly thirty minutes from the time of his call, was the team. Gage had a large file of operatives to choose from, and he usually stuck to his core team with a few specialists. This time, he chose three core members and two specialists since what they were dealing with could become a bit tricky.

"Good afternoon, Banner," Gage addressed the large, hulking woman before him. She had spoken first, as always, and had Gage's complete trust. Banner was six-and-a-half-feet tall, well-muscled, and deadly. She was Gage's second in command, level-headed, and probably the only woman outside of Rylene that Gage truly loved. He'd never tell her that, and she would never admit to feeling the same way. He trusted her implicitly.

Gage handed Banner the file and addressed the remaining four team members. He would bring six into the job, and six would come out, just like always.

"Banner will disseminate the site and job information to you before we leave, but we need to get some introductions out of the way."

Gage stopped in front of a small man. He had large eyes, big ears, and perpetually sniffled as if he had a cold from birth. This was bio-material specialist Mickey Riggs. Gage smiled as Riggs wiped his nose of on his own sleeve. The young man smiled back, flashing those trademark yellowed teeth.

"Mickey Riggs, biologist. If he sneezes, duck."

Riggs chuckled along with the rest of the group.

Gage moved down the line, stopping in front a tall man dressed in white. He looked to be antiseptic, especially in comparison to Riggs. This was medical specialist, Dr. Hasan McKay. He tried to stare straight ahead, but every sniffle and scratch from Riggs drew McKay's eyes toward him, wary of whatever diseases the biologist carried with him at any time. McKay turned and pleaded to Gage with his eyes.

"Go ahead, Doc," Gage told the man.

With a sigh of relief, McKay moved to the end of the line, putting a full two people in front of him and Riggs.

"Better, Doc?" Gage asked.

"Yessir."

The rest of the group, including Riggs, laughed out loud. They had seen this play out in varying ways before.

"Dr. Hasan McKay, folks, and our medical specialist. Being uncomfortable next to Riggs is his way of telling us he knows what he is doing."

The group laughed again, and Gage pulled up in front of

a small woman. She was stocky and the perpetual scowl, even while laughing, made her even more ominous. One name, one purpose: Vasquez and security.

"You all know Vasquez, I assume. She did the extensive background checks and physical appraisals on everyone in this room."

"I want to object one more time, sir." Vasquez stood straight and faced forward. She was ex-military, like Gage, but relished the discipline and hierarchy. Gage respected that even if he didn't agree.

"Noted." Vasquez wasn't the biggest fan of the final member of the team. Admittedly, Gage wasn't happy with the final member either, but he was the best mechanical engineer that Gage had ever encountered. He was also shallow, headstrong, and had authority issues. Although a genius, he had a habit of making dangerous situations even more dangerous through reckless behavior... but his skill set was exactly what they needed.

"She means me, right?" David Gage stage whispered loud enough for most of the galaxy to hear. The Colonel's younger brother just couldn't help himself.

"Yes, David." Gage moved on quickly, adding, "David is our mechanical engineer, and what we will be up against will require his participation."

"Asshole," Vasquez said, not quietly enough.

David turned and laughed. Vasquez tried to hold it together but just couldn't stomach David's impudence. She turned and had a fist cocked, ready to lay the smug bastard out.

Before anything could happen, Banner was between the two and holding them aloft by the neck. Suspended a few inches off the ground by the scruff of the neck was a universe-wide violence deterrent.

"Are we kosher?" Banner asked.

Vasquez managed to grunt something and David pouted. That was enough, and Banner dropped the two to the ground.

"Thank you, Banner," Gage said.

"Yessir."

"That's the scoop, folks. Let's get geared up and on the ship. Banner will brief you on the location and what we are looking at before we go into chyro-sleep."

Riggs raised his hand. Gage pointed to him.

"Sir, where are we going?"

"Centauri Six."

All of them, aside from Banner, moaned loudly.

David leaned over to Vasquez. "Better pack that long underwear."

Vasquez gritted her teeth and ignored the comment as best she could. The team broke up to get ready.

Banner called out. "We are gear up in twenty, people. Mark it!" She turned to Gage. "Is your brother the wisest choice?"

"Only choice." Gage wished it were otherwise, but he needed a certified miracle worker on this one.

"The file says that after the initial alarm it was manually shut off, but there hasn't been any communication from the installation." Banner held up the file. "Not much info here."

"Right."

"Are we looking for survivors? Containing the threat? Eliminating the threat?"

Gage turned and looked at the only person he trusted in the world, outside his daughter. "I don't expect too much of a problem, but the lack of communication bugs me. I want you to get with Riggs—"

"Oh, God."

"I didn't say sleep with him, just stand next to him, and

get an idea of what they may have been doing bio-wise on that rock. The client wasn't forthcoming."

"Shit."

"Yep."

Banner saluted Gage and turned to find Riggs.

Gage watched her go. He had his reservations about this one but those had to wait. They had a job to do.

CHAPTER FOUR

The ship touched down on Centauri Six seventy-two hours after the initial call was made by the client to Gage. The chyro pods had opened while the ship was in orbit, the team shook off the remainder of the sleep sickness, a common procedure as the ship descended.

When Gage had started in the business, the only ship he could afford as an independent contractor allowed him to basically mop up whatever slop work he could get his hands on in Earth's solar system. He had met Banner then, and she had been with him ever since. This was immediately post-divorce, and he was grateful for the diversion. As the two of them built a reputation, the work increased, and so did the funds. He graduated to a ship with chyro-sleep possibilities and light speed capabilities. That opened up the entire system for Gage.

The chyro was necessary since the light speed process was still too much for any human to endure, and as the manifest destiny of the species pushed them farther into space, it was necessary to safely transport humans. The first few experiments in waking light speed travel were whispered about in space travel circles as driving the participants stark raving mad. No one knows for sure anymore, and that myth could have been started by the chyro-sleep manufacturers. Either way, better safe than sorry.

The team was jovial with one another, David being the usual exception, as they prepped for landfall. Centauri VI grew larger and larger as the ship descended. Banner piloted the manual take offs and landing but the on-board pilot took care of the rest.

As was his routine, Gage went over the documents before landing. Banner could tell he was upset with the lack of information, but she was the only one. The rest of the team joked and chided one another, with even David joining in… at least tangentially. Gage regretted the fact that his little brother was such a pariah on these missions. The kid was a genius, legitimately, and Gage had seen him pull off certified mechanical miracles. The death of their parents was tough on him, though. Gage had been older at twenty, and a thirteen-year-old David living with him produced a fair amount of animosity. He loved his brother, though, and just hoped that one day they could work through it.

Despite David's participation, Gage smiled. He had come a long way from cleaning up radiation leaks from poorly made domestic power units and shepherding child-sized rodents to the sweet hereafter in urban Earth tenements. His own ship. His own team. His pick of jobs. This particular client always paid very well, so Gage would routinely accept the offer without looking at the specs. As they touched down on Centauri VI, that little pang of annoyance cropped up again, and he scowled. Forewarned is forearmed.

Gage's deep thought was interrupted by the loud landing siren. The lighting in the ship shifted to blue, indicating take-off or landing, and the siren blared throughout. Banner's voice barked orders over the intercom.

"Suit up, suckers. Our destination is currently experiencing a heatwave at negative 30 degrees. We will have approximately sixty seconds of surface time before making it to the compound. Standard exit and approach."

Gage stood up. Ready or not, he thought, here we come.

The ship landed smoothly and easily like always, and the team disembarked, led by Gage. Banner always took the rear and sealed the ship with her security code, a bio-metric hand print. Gage had an override code, of course, but he could never remember what it was anyway. He owned the ship, but she made it purr. The rest of the team, stuffed inside the survival suits, shambled toward the dock of the installation.

The suits they wore were standard issue and designed for the harshest conditions. Even with the state of the art insulation and breathing apparatus, there was a short shelf life while using the suits on a planet like Centauri VI. Actually, no one had ever explored the survivability limit, preferring to spend as little time as possible on landscapes like this. Vasquez, Banner, and Gage all carried weapons. Banner and Gage sported handheld cannons that fired heated bolts of plasma. Vasquez, of course, carried a large rifle version. That was the official weapon count. Gage knew his security expert and would bet that she had a few more toys tucked away.

The docking bay was a standard issue one. Once the initial equipment load-in happened, all deliveries were of the standard supplies variety. There was a large door that could encompass a ground unit, but nothing that the ship could have entered directly. Even if it was large enough, the lack of communication from the compound wouldn't have gotten the bay open.

Gage waved David to the front of the group as they approached the door. He trudged forward, knocking his shoulder into Gage as he moved past. The colonel shook his head and let it go. That was the price of dealing with David.

David took a moment to inspect the control panel.

"What's it look like, David?" Gage asked. He was always a little surprised how mechanical the suit's speaker made him sound.

"A door." Classic David.

"And?"

With a sigh, David turned to his brother. "We're lucky; the power is still functioning in the compound. Shouldn't take long."

"Good," Vasquez said from the middle of the group. "I know I can't feel how cold it is with this thing on, but I am starting to feel how cold it is."

Riggs laughed and sniffled in his suit, fogging the visor up.

David hunkered over the control panel as the wind whistled. Gage was beginning to understand what Vasquez meant. Just being here chilled him to the bone no matter what kind of protection they were under.

The group shuffled as the seconds wore into a full minute. They pressed in tighter together. Just as Gage was about to ask for an updated ETA, the door hissed open, rising up and allowing access to the compound.

David turned and bowed, gesturing for the team to enter.

Gage nodded and hefted his weapon and clicked on the sighting light. It cut through the darkened loading bay to reveal standard operating nothing. Gage entered, followed by the rest of the team.

The loading dock itself was unremarkable. As Banner entered, David scooted over to the corresponding control panel on the inside and shut the bay door, again with a hiss. The silence was pervasive. Only the faintest howls of the wind could be heard outside, buffeting the side of the compound relentlessly.

Without a sound, McKay had an environmental sensor out gauging the atmosphere. It lit up green with a squeak, and he nodded.

"Conditions are habitable. The temperature is a bit

elevated, a little warmer than the compound should be kept, but the air is rich."

Gage nodded. "All right, folks, shuck 'em."

The team responded by taking the suits off. The team protocol was followed to a tee. McKay collected each of the suits, inspected them for damages, and then left them in a secluded spot to the left of the bay door on a table.

"How we doin', Doc?"

"Ready for a quick exit, sir. "

Gage nodded. He motioned for Banner. She joined him at the front of the group.

"OK, we need to see what is happening here." Gage pointed to the lone access tunnel leading from the bay. "That should get us to the central complex area—the bunker. We can set up shop in the command center and go from there."

Banner nodded.

Before she could turn and relay the information to the team, the very access tunnel door that Gage pointed at literally blew off its hinges. The large, metal door, designed to withstand a great deal of abuse, clanged across the floor before skidding to a halt against the opposite wall.

Gage and the team turned slowly. Smoke billowed from the tunnel, and as it cleared figures took shape.

"Weapons up!" Gage called out.

Vasquez and Banner joined him as Riggs and McKay hung back. Before Gage could argue, David pulled a plasma hand cannon from his pack and moved next to his brother.

"What the hell?"

David shrugged. "I never believed in your no-weapon policy for specialists."

"*Un-trained* specialists."

"Whatever."

Whispering from the tunnel drew Gage's attention. Emerging from the smoke were five humans dressed in the security uniforms of the compound. Gage noticed that David and the others noticeably relaxed upon seeing them. He did not. What he heard didn't match what he saw.

"Weapons UP!" Gage called out again.

"Andy, it's the damn security detail," David said, holstering his weapon. He stepped forward and extended his hand. "We are glad to see you guys!"

The whispering had grown louder and now that Gage could hear it better, he recognized it as… hissing. The security detail was definitely hissing. Different tones and levels, back and forth, but hissing.

Before Gage could yell out to his brother, David caught the vibe and backed up quickly next to his brother.

Undaunted, the security detail lurched forward. They moved awkwardly, as if they were struggling to get used to their own bodies.

"Stand down. State your name and intent," Gage said to the group although he didn't expect a response. The detail hissed and continued forward.

"Colonel?" Banner said it, but everyone was thinking it.

Gage waited until they were nearly on top of them. The hissing was one thing, but Gage needed to see. When they were close enough, he got what he wanted. Their eyes were shiny… moist… and their skin was pale and had blue veins running throughout. The security detail was compromised, and as they raised their hands to attack, hostile.

"They're compromised. Light 'em up!" Gage announced. It didn't please him or any of them, but the team followed the orders.

Banner, Vasquez, David, and Gage fired with precision, with his brother quietly impressing the Colonel. Bolts of hot plasma struck each of the detail, putting them down quickly.

The team lowered their weapons, and Gage was about to direct Riggs and McKay give them the once over, when the hissing started again. The security detail struggled to their feet and started moving forward again.

"What the hell, Chief?" Vasquez asked, her eyes wide.

Gage was speechless. They had fired precise and true; his team was good. This wasn't supposed to happen.

"Take them down. Extreme prejudice."

The weapons raised again, and the team fired bolt after bolt into the shambling detail. As the impossible pushed forward, the shooters were pushed back. Gage changed tactics and instead of shooting for the core of the assailant, took a shot at the head. It took a moment to get through the protective layers of the security helmets, but it did. The officer in front of him took one more bolt, sizzling through his frontal lobe, and dropped to the floor like his puppet strings were cut.

"Raise levels. Headshots only, and take the brain out!" Gage called out.

The team responded without a word, dispatching each of the detail quickly. Once down, the smell of burning flesh and gray matter permeated the room. David gagged a bit and the rest wanted to, but they choked it back.

Gage stepped forward. He toed the first corpse, rocking what used to be the head of the compounds security detail. After determining the thing was dead, Gage motioned for McKay and Riggs.

"Doc, Riggs… I need to find out what was running these things. You saw them, it looked like they were being piloted."

Riggs whistled. "Parasite? Telepathy? Damn. What happened?"

McKay ducked down and took the first body under the arms. With Riggs help, he moved the body onto a wheeled cart used for deliveries.

"What happened?" Vasquez parroted Riggs as she walked by, strapping a handheld plasma gun to her opposite side and loading more weaponry. "Shit just got real is what happened!"

Gage looked down the hallway, knowing he could never see the bunker, but giving it a shot. "We still need to get to that bunker. McKay and Riggs, grab a weapon from Vasquez, and set up shop in here. We don't have time to find the medical bay before we know what we're cleaning here."

David snorted. "Aren't they untrained?"

Gage didn't bother looking at him. "I'm changing my opinion on specialists. Everyone else, let's get into standard formation and hit that hallway. It is about 20 yards to the main common area, and at one point this complex had sixty staff members total. We don't know how many are—"

"Zombies?" David interrupted.

"No such thing, and quit watching that shit; it'll rot your brain. We don't know how many are compromised, so stay on point. Let's move out."

Gage took a deep breath and took point in front of the doorway, smoke still billowing. The team filled in behind him: David, Vasquez, and Banner.

Banner looked back at Riggs and McKay. "Colonel?"

"Banner."

"Should we leave McKay and Riggs here alone?"

Gage turned and watched the two begin the standard argument as they worked. He sighed. They were defenseless on a good day. "Good idea. Banner, stay behind and see if you can help. We'll call when we reach the bunker and secure that. Once the medical bay is secured, we move them in there."

Banner nodded. "Roger."

Banner left the line, and Vasquez stepped back, filling in. Her attitude more than making up for Banner's size.

Gage grinned. "Let's do this."

They plunged in.

CHAPTER FIVE

Gage, David, and Vasquez inched down the hallway. As he had indicated, they didn't have very far to go to reach the central hub area. From there, if all went well, they could get into the command center and see if any data on the breech was recorded. Any aid they could get in regard to exactly what they would run in to would help.

The Colonel wiped his brow with a shirt sleeve. The hall was muggy, and it carried a very thick humidity.

"David," Gage said. "What kind of malfunction would account for the current temp and saturation?"

David shook his head, straining to see through the smoke and dark to try and get a drop on what may be in front of them.

"Nothing, sir."

Gage grimaced. Now was not the time for shenanigans. He sneered, and that sneer came out in his voice. "I understand that. Just answer the damn question."

"I did! If there was a malfunction in the temp then it would go in the opposite direction. It would just shut down, and then the entire complex would match the exterior. This is on purpose."

Gage stopped and turned. Vasquez looked up at David, too.

"As in, intentional?" Gage asked.

David nodded.

Shaking his head, Gage turned back to the lead and foraged further. He needed to find out what kind of organism this was stat. If it needed humidity, that usually meant it was growing. Nothing grows in the cold, after all.

They approached the hatch to the common area. According to the plans, this was the central hub. Across the main area, including the two stories of sleeper units, was the kitchen, mess hall, and central command that held the administrative offices. It was a good sign that the security detail had to blow the door off its hinges to get to Gage's crew. That meant one of two things: the thing that was controlling those men wanted the element of surprise, or it didn't have control of the admin area. Gage obviously preferred the latter.

Inside, the command center was dark. What little light shone through the large windows were obviously component LED and other ancillary lights. The atmosphere was still intact, but that could be adjusted from the engineering section at the top of the complex. This command center was hexagonal and featured windows that allowed visual access in 360 degrees. It was the center of the compound, and the halls to the labs, like spokes, radiated from there. This ground floor held the common areas, and the residential areas were on the upper floors. All of it controlled from here.

Gage nodded to David. Without a word, David slid toward the access panel to the door and went to work. Vasquez followed and turned, putting her back against David's while he worked. She scanned the area for threats. There was nothing aside from the smoke and an eerie, pervasive quiet.

Gage tried to ignore the heat and moved around the perimeter of the control center, peering in the windows and looking for signs of anything that would compromise the plan or jeopardize their lives. He noticed nothing as David finished.

"Bingo," David said and stepped back, drawing his weapon.

Vasquez turned, and Gage fell in beside her. The door to the control center hissed open and Gage entered. It was empty.

David went right to work trying to find out what was

happening to the system. Vasquez kept watch and Gage accessed the command center's back-up activity database using the codes from the client.

The three of them turned as a hologram of the camera footage shimmered to life in the middle of the room. Gage dialed it back to just before the communications went dead. The hologram showed the view from the command center, complete with two frantic technicians that had barricaded themselves in. Surrounding the command center were a minimum of fifteen individuals in security uniforms, lab coats, maintenance uniforms, etc. Their movements, that stilted shuffle, were reminiscent of the group that attacked Gage's team.

The image jumped to the mess hall area where two lab-coated individuals, a man and a woman, pulled mechanical gear through the dining area and into the kitchen.

"David, what is that gear?" Gage asked.

David squinted at the image. "Not sure. It resembles exo-skeletal gear for mining, but smaller."

Gage and David looked at one another.

"The suit?" Gage finally said.

David nodded, and they both turned back to the holo-gram. It switched again – to the residential areas. Nothing. Medical bay. Nothing. More switches, from lab to lab. There were no individuals in the labs, not a single one. The labs themselves varied, though. Some were thoroughly destroyed, ransacked, and others were untouched.

Gage had the sneaking suspicion that what the client didn't tell them could fill volumes.

The hologram switched again, back to the command center. The group was gone and the command center was empty, just like they had found it.

Vasquez shook her head. "I don't like this, boss."

Gage nodded his head. "I'm feeling a little nervous

myself. Let me get Banner on this, too." Gage grabbed his communicator and dialed upped the docking bay. "Banner, this is Gage."

"Go for Banner," the communicator squawked back.

"We're in the center. It looks abandoned. We have some holos of compromised scientists using the mess hall as a base for what looks like the mechanized suit construction. It appears that the bio-organism used for the suit has—"

"Woken up?" David offered, looking up from where he was plugging away at the command center console.

Gage shrugged. "Yeah, woken up, I guess. It appears to have some parasitic qualities, and we know that it can control at least six humans at once."

"Got that, Chief," Banner answered back. "We've found some interesting things here, too. The parasite that Riggs and McKay pulled out and off of this guy is unique. Like the document says, it appears to fully oxygenate the victim and gets through to the brain and sets up shop. We'll know more soon."

"Good," Gage radioed back. "We definitely get the feeling the command center is a bust. The medical bay looks to have been empty at the time of the crisis; we'll check out there."

"Roger."

Gage turned. Vasquez stared at him, eyes wide in panic.

"This is no good, sir. No bueno." Vasquez wiped her brow to punctuate the statement.

Gage nodded. He gave her a pat on the shoulder and turned to his brother. "Make any sense out of this?"

David turned. He wanted to be glib, but the evidence was too bizarre. "It looks as if all the environmental controls were routed from here to the kitchen. So, that looks like it is where the thing set up shop."

Vasquez walked the perimeter of the control center like a

watch dog on patrol. She was getting more and more aggravated.

"Why not the medical bay?" Gage asked.

David shrugged his shoulders. "From what it says here, the environmental controls are standardized in the bay if there is a malfunction. Makes sense."

Gage nodded. "All right. Let's head back to Banner and see whether they are in finding a way to fight this thing."

"Finally! Something to do!" Vasquez turned, holding her weapon high.

Gage turned to David. "What do you think they are doing in there with the gear and the environment controls?"

"Making an army. There has to be a reason it needs the bio-mech, though."

Vasquez punched the door panel and waited for it to hiss up. Nothing. She hit it again. Still nothing. She turned back and looked at Gage and David, eyes wide.

"Don't look at me," David said. "I got it open the first time."

Before Gage could chastise his brother, and before Vasquez could call him a bastard, the exterior of the command center was filled with lurching, moaning bodies. The team had their weapons up and were ready for action, but there had to be fifteen compromised humans pounding on the glass. Dressed in lab coats, sleepwear, and janitorial staff uniforms, each of the assailants had the same glassy look as the initial attackers. Gage even recognized the two people that held center from the holo video earlier. He lifted the communicator, ready to convey the situation to Banner.

CHAPTER SIX

Riggs and McKay fascinated Banner. They worked together, pouring over the body of a security officer barely cognizant of the world around them. The entire complex could have exploded at that point and they would be none the wiser, yet they could bicker like a married couple.

"Do you see this? The organism covered the entire body like a thin sheen," Riggs said before stifling a sneeze on his sleeve. He used forceps to pull the gelatinous substance away from the face of the corpse and let it snap back.

McKay snatched the tool from his hand and tsked his disapproval. "Do you see what you've done? It's split along the side of the face here. You could have compromised..." McKay stopped short. He looked at Riggs.

Riggs looked at McKay. They appeared to share a thought. Banner laughed to herself. The pasty white Riggs, short and diseased, stared up at the clinically sterile and olive-skinned McKay, and they shared a mind.

"It died," McKay said. "The host lost communication, and it died."

"So the control is temporary, or did it do it on purpose?"

"Gage mentioned the gear... it isn't perfect!"

"It isn't perfect!"

The pair of them high-fived. Banner stepped in, looking for a translation.

"OK, I need to tell Gage. What isn't perfect?"

McKay went to speak and thought twice. He motioned to Riggs. Riggs shook his head and motioned to McKay.

"You first; it was yours," Riggs said and sniffled.

"I couldn't," McKay countered. "The forceps test was key to this."

Normally Banner loved to hear the banter, but time was of the essence. "Stop it. McKay, what isn't perfect?"

He smiled. "The organism. It looks like it doesn't have full control. From what we can tell, it covers the host, giving it oxygen and sustenance, and takes the frontal cortex through the nose. The parasite is remote and functions like a hive mind."

Banner nodded. "Yes, yes, been there. What isn't perfect?"

"It can't hold it! That is why it needs the relays, the mechanics, the environment. Right now it is putting together the prototype suit just like the complex was built for."

"Using the humidity to replicate pieces of itself to compromise the human workers," Riggs threw in.

"Right! The organism can use the people, but it isn't permanent. It is making the suit so it can live; bond it to the host structure. It's thinking and using the collected resources of those scientists to do it."

Banner looked around the room. From the docking bay door to the access port that Gage and the rest of the team took. The security detail littered on the floor sealed the deal. She smacked her own head. She pulled her weapon as she went for the communicator. What it really wanted was sitting right outside that door.

Then all hell broke loose. Banner's head snapped to the side as the sound of many, many shuffling feet filled the hallway. She hefted her weapon and barked orders to Riggs and McKay. She didn't need to translate the look on their faces to know that they were useless in a fight.

"You two!" she yelled while pointing, hoping to get them settled before the horde arrived. "Pick a corpse and get underneath. Stay quiet."

"What?" Riggs asked.

Banner turned and glared. "Now. Under a body!"

McKay pushed Riggs toward a corpse. The pair awkwardly got onto the ground and pulled a body over them. Banner watched, turning only when she felt that the boys were covered adequately. She hefted the pistol and took a deep breath as a group of compromised humans shuffled out of the darkness of the hall and straight at her.

They moved as one, like some kind of single-celled organism. She fired into the chest of the lead, formerly a human being in a lab coat. She could see the layer of organism burn away at the point of impact but replace itself quickly. She remembered the head shots and adjusted accordingly. There was enough time to pop off two quick plasma bursts into the leader's head, burning through the organism, the front of the skull, and then into the frontal lobe. It smelled like burning liver on a stove, and the leader dropped only to be trampled by the remainder of the group.

The horde shoved forward, still as one, and were on her. She swung the butt of the pistol, crashing into the skull of what was once a janitor named Szagesh, if the name tag was accurate. The heavy metal handle and grip, powered by Banner, crashed in and through the skull. Banner was showered in blood, organism, and brain matter. She swung around, her fist connecting with the jaw of another lab-coated automaton. It had no effect. No matter how powerful she was, the numbers simply overcame her, and with a strangled cry, she was buried in thrashing flesh.

From underneath one of the corpses, Riggs could see the entire event play out. Like a horde of some carnivorous beetle swarming a piece of meat, the shambling group covered her, and as quickly as they came in, they disappeared, taking Banner with them. Riggs stared ahead and blinked, processing what he had just seen.

Riggs looked around, making sure that the horde had completely left. With a great deal of effort, he pushed the corpse off and stood up.

"McKay," he whispered.

A corpse on the other side of the room shuddered.

"McKay, they're gone!" Riggs said a bit louder.

"Are you sure?" From under the corpse.

"Yes, they took Banner!"

The corpse shuddered again and slid to the side. McKay's head popped up and looked around. "They took Banner?"

Riggs nodded.

"Why?"

Riggs shook his head, looking around the room. "We need weapons and have to get ahold of Gage."

"Agreed. Why would they take her?"

Riggs looked at the hallway and sniffled. He wiped the snot on his sleeve. He stood for a moment, thinking. After a moment he turned to McKay. "Because they're smart, that's why!"

"That doesn't help much, Riggs, if they're..." McKay stopped mid-sentence. He followed Riggs epiphany.

"See?"

"Oh, my God. We need Gage."

Riggs nodded. "We should have seen it coming."

McKay joined Riggs in looking around the room. Mounted on the wall was what looked like the answer to a prayer. He walked over and pulled the cold fire extinguisher from the wall. McKay held it up and turned to Riggs. "Hey!"

Riggs smiled. "Let's find another one. Gage needs to know this stuff."

CHAPTER SEVEN

Gage, David, and Vasquez look around them as the small cracks in the command center windows grew larger and longer as the group of former staff pushed forward. By last count, Gage had fifteen assailants. They managed to take out six in the bay, but had one more weapon holder in Banner.

Gage held the communicator up as it played static.

"Banner?" Vasquez asked.

Gage shrugged his shoulders. He turned to David. "You ready for this? We need to get to the bay."

David didn't have a witty comeback. He knew how much Banner meant to his brother

With a sigh, Gage stepped toward the door.

David shook his head. "I can't get it open; the controls have been rerouted."

Gage aimed his weapon at the control panel. "I'm going to do this manually… on three."

"One." Vasquez readied her rifle, lifting it to her shoulder.

"Two." David took a deep breath. The horde continued to press in on them. The windows cracked even more.

"Three," Gage said and fired. The blast ripped into the panel, and it erupted in fire. The lights went red in the command center, the siren blared, and the door flew upward.

The horde immediately pressed forward. With a scream, Vasquez opened fire. The high-powered rifle shot plasma bolt after plasma bolt. She sheared off limbs, and they fell to the ground sizzling, holes burned in chests, and heads exploded in molten brain matter.

Vasquez fired and moved forward, David and Gage behind her, firing as well. The mob pressed back a bit, opening a pocket for them to move just outside of the command center.

For each of the lab coats and uniforms that went down, another one took its spot. Gage fired as fast as he could but could only think that the initial assessment of the numbers of the horde may have been understated.

Vasquez stopped shooting. Like a well-oiled machined, she slipped between Gage and David as they took the lead.

"I'm out. I need to re-charge!" Vasquez shouted. She slung the rifle over her shoulder and pulled a long knife from her belt.

Gage took a quick look at his pistol's levels and grimaced. He was almost out, too, and knew that David had to be close. As he and David shot, Vasquez would pop up and around his shoulders, sticking the things with her knife. She managed to get one right between eyes, and the thing dropped. So they knew it was all about the brain.

David stopped firing and spun the gun around, using it as a club. Gage fired his last two shots and did the same thing.

The space that the trio had carved filled with the horde quickly. The three of them slashed out with knives and bashed with makeshift clubs, but the mob slowly took more ground.

"It's been a pleasure," Gage said between blows.

David turned to his brother, tears filled his eyes. "I'm sorry."

Gage looked at his brother quickly. "What?"

David slammed his gun into the head of mess hall worker, complete with hairnet. "I'm sorry for being such a…"

"Not here. Not now," Gage said, cutting his brother off. "This isn't the end."

David shook his head and smiled, swinging away.

The horde moved in closer. The three of them could feel fingers pulling at their faces, their clothes being torn.

Faintly, from the hallway, Gage could hear something. It was real language, not the moaning and sounds the things made. If Gage didn't know any better, it sounded like bickering. His thoughts evaporated a moment later. Vasquez fired, taking the top off of a scientist's head and showering the horde in brains and blood. David continued to fight, firing and pushing forward. Gage fought as well, but the three of them were quickly pinned against the control center, and it looked as if the end was finally near. Hands, teeth, and heads pressed on the three of them.

"Is now the right time?" David managed through gritted teeth.

"Maybe," Gage answered.

The press of angry, parasite-infested flesh intensified when, closer, Gage was sure he heard two voices snapping at one another like an old married couple, each snarky quip punctuated by the sound of an exhaust port or steam pipe blowing out.

"I told you, aim higher! We'll never get there in time!" the first voice said.

"Shut up, and just let me do it."

"Always. You're always like this when you 'man up.'"

Gage thought he recognized the voices. When one of them sneezed; that sealed the deal.

"Riggs! McKay! We're pinned here!"

The exhaust sound fired off again and again. Even as a finger latched onto Vasquez' ear and teeth sunk into David they felt as if the press lessened a bit. The trio watched in disbelief as the horde fell off one after the other, as if they were being peeled off layer by layer. Each time one of the compromised dropped, the sound of that steam pipe exhaust echoed in the chamber.

Finally, only four of the horde were left in front of Gage, David, and Vasquez. What looked like smoke cleared, and through the haze they could see Riggs and McKay holding a cold fire extinguisher. McKay was the triggerman and held it up.

"Empty, guys!"

Vasquez sneered and hefted the rifle. "I'm not."

Finally gaining enough separation between the horde and her rifle, Vasquez fired into the face of a janitor, and it exploded in front of them. Before Gage or anyone could react, Vasquez had fired three more times, catching the compromised in the head. The bodies dropped to the floor, sizzling, and the room was filled with the smell of burned flesh.

Riggs dropped to his knees, hovering over the final victim of Vasquez' rage, and watched the organism itself shrink away from the sizzling brain matter. It hardened before his very eyes.

Gage turned to Vasquez. "That was... final."

She smiled and slung the rifle over her shoulder. David stepped up, hand held and ready for a high five. Reluctantly, and suppressing a smile, Vasquez slapped hands with him. She then went right to her damaged ear, and David slapped a hand around the nasty-looking bite wound.

Gage turned to McKay and shook his hand. "Where did you get the idea?"

"It's the cold. This is a cold extinguisher, the chemical mimics a temperature drop. The organism hates the cold—"

"Hence the rain forest feeling," Gage said.

"Yes! We've found some interesting things out about the organisms!"

"Banner?"

McKay opened his mouth to speak but stammered. His exuberance left quickly.

Gage stepped forward. "McKay. Where's Banner? Is she...?"

Riggs stood forward, wiping his nose on his sleeve. "We don't think so. We think she's part of its plan."

Gage stood and stared at his science department. He was joined by Vasquez and David. The three of them had a single look, but only David could vocalize it.

"Wait. The mind-control amoeba has a plan?"

Riggs and McKay nodded.

"And it needed Banner?" Vasquez asked.

Again, they answered in the affirmative. The group stood there, silently.

"Well?" Gage finally asked.

Riggs and McKay looked at one another as if they were playing a silent game of Rochambeau. Riggs turned to Gage; apparently he won.

"We believe that the organism has a plan to get off the planet."

Gage shook his head, trying to take it in. "What does that have to do with Banner? How did an organism come up with a plan like that, anyway?"

McKay took over. "We think that it is evolving with each host. Taking over these people has allowed it to... grow. Intellectually."

"It's getting smarter," David said.

McKay nodded. "It's already pretty smart. We think that the plan was to draw us here specifically because it wants off the planet, and it needs a host—a particular host."

"We found out that it can't handle the extreme cold planet side, so it needs a ship and a host body that can..." Riggs petered off. He couldn't look Gage in the eye.

Gage stepped forward, taking Riggs by the shoulders and forcing him to look up. "Look, I can take it. She means a lot to me, and we need to help her. Why Banner?"

Riggs sighed. "Banner's physique is unique. McKay and I believe that she is the only one that could survive the process of attaching the bio-mechanical aspects of the suit to the host body so the organism can have complete control. This would then augment the host body and make the organism..."

"One tough son of a bitch," Vasquez whispered.

The rest of them just stood there as McKay and Riggs nodded.

Gage looked up. "What do you mean survive?"

Before Riggs could answer, the horde lying on the ground

shifted. One moaned... then the other. An arm shot up in the air. A body moved.

Gage looked to McKay and Riggs, his eyes wide.

"Oh, yeah," McKay said, shrugging his shoulders. "The effects of the cold extinguisher are temporary."

Gage shook his head. He pointed down the hall. "Back to the ship. We need to stock up, and then we are going to get extract Banner."

"What about the client?" David asked as they started down the hall.

Gage snarled. "They can nuke the place for all I care."

CHAPTER EIGHT

Banner's eyes fluttered open, and she closed them immediately. The harsh, white industrial lights burned at first. She squinted after a moment and could tell that she was in the kitchen. As they suspected, steam hung in the room, and the atmosphere was swampy. *Score one for the big brains*, she thought. She slowly became used to the harsh light and opened her eyes fully. She was restrained in some manner, but was upright and facing what appeared to be the industrial ovens. Her head and neck were tied down, as well as her limbs and torso, so she was effectively going nowhere. She could tell that they had stripped her and she lay there, tied down and naked.

The sounds of people—or something—entering the room caught her off guard, and Banner tried to turn her head. The restraints were tight, and she cried out as they pinched the side of her head. She vocalized more out of surprise than pain, but it resulted in one of the lab workers, obviously compromised by the organism, to shuffle over. She looked at the man and then down too see the name tag on his coat: RIZZOWSKI and recognized it from the file. This used to be the geneticist. From what she could see, he looked like he used to be a prick, so she figured he was the cause of all these issues. Rizzowski's skin reflected the harsh lights in an odd manner, like there was a greasy sheen.

Rizzowski looked into her eyes, inspected her mouth, and pretty much cased Banner's entire body as if she were some new sort of acquisition at the zoo. After thinking about it for a moment, she laughed out loud at the thought. She was the new animal.

Rizzowski looked up quickly from wherever he was examining.

Banner smiled. "You should take a vid, it lasts longer," she said. The bravado helped to hide the unmitigated fear.

Rizzowski cocked its head. He opened his mouth, trying to mimic speech, but only a gurgle came out. As Banner watched, it appeared as if a piece of Rizzowski's face detached and reached out for her. She recoiled as far as she could as the organism shot out a tendril. It stroked her cheek and extended down, making its way along the rope-like veins in her neck down and over her breasts. She clamped her mouth shut and pursed her lips, determined to never give this thing the satisfaction of showing her real disgust and contempt.

The tendril grew and continued down her abdomen, feeling the tight, well-developed abdominal muscles. Rizzowski's head stayed upright, eye to eye with her, as the organism explored around Banner's vagina and powerful thighs. She struggled to hold in her revulsion.

The tendril recoiled, joining the rest of Rizzowski's face, and Banner remembered to breathe for the first time since that thing started the exploration.

Rizzowski turned as another lab-coated formerly-sentient human approached. It was a woman, petite but pretty. She was carrying a piece of the exo-suit in one hand and what looked like small needles with filament wires running from them. Banner recognized the exo piece from the file, but was unsure what the filament had to do with it.

The woman and Rizzowski worked in tandem, as if they were part of the same body, and Banner realized they really were. She had the same bright sheen. If Riggs and McKay were right, then the humidity and environment in the kitchen would allow the organism to grow, breed, and have a more of a complete control.

Banner tried to look down but could not, of course, as she felt the woman's hand on her outside thigh. A cold piece of metal, the exo piece she assumed, was held against her thigh. Directly across from her, Rizzowski reached into his lab coat pocket and pulled out a handheld cauterizer. Banner's eyes went wide. She was familiar with the tool; it was a common first aid item that allowed people to quickly cauterize a wound to stop bleeding, close an opening, and when in deft hands, graft biological materials together. Rizzowski was a geneticist, so by extrapolation, the organism was not a geneticist. Rizzowski clicked on the cauterizer and it hummed. She could see the tip glow as the compromised scientist ducked, disappearing from her line of sight.

Banner figured out the plan right before they started. The exo-suit was one thing, but it wouldn't work unless the suit was tied into the bio-metrics of the organism. Each one of those filaments would need to be hard-wired into the bio material; that was the original intent. Now, the organism could avoid any issues like that by simply grafting the exo-suit to the chosen host body, and once it was complete, inhabit the host without experiencing any of the pain.

She gritted her teeth at the thought. By Banner's estimation, and from what the file said, the relays required could number in the thousands. The sound of the cauterizer was reminiscent of a short electrical charge, and Banner smelled the burned skin before she felt the intense, mind-numbing pain of a relay being grafted directly to a nerve. She couldn't scream, she couldn't do anything. The pain shot up her leg and wracked her entire body. As Banner convulsed within the restraints, one thought did clearly come break through the fog of pain: That was only the first one.

CHAPTER NINE

Gage held court in the docking bay. Laid out before them on one of the tables was what remained of their weaponry. Vasquez' rifle, David and Gage's side-arms, and two more of the cold extinguishers joined what Gage had pulled from the bodies of the security detail. This added three more plasma hand cannons and one baton.

Gage looked up at his crew. David, Vasquez, McKay, and Riggs all stared back. He knew that look. That was the, 'What the hell do we do now?' look. Gage cleared his throat and pointed to the table. "Pick your poison."

Vasquez pulled her rifle back, one of the security hand guns, and the baton. David chuckled to himself, avoiding Vasquez' glare, and chose his own handgun. McKay and Riggs each grabbed a fire extinguisher. Gage motioned to his brother, offering a security handgun to him. David shrugged and pointed at his left arm and the new bandage that leaked blood despite the care taken in patching him up.

"Bum wing," David said.

Gage nodded and took both the pistols. He took a deep breath and then addressed the crew. "Our main priority is getting Banner, and from what McKay and Riggs have said, she may be compromised." No one looked at him as he said that, and Gage knew why. Banner was a friend. A colleague. "I think our best plan is to incapacitate the workers here. By our count, there are still around thirty... give or take. We reload on the extinguishers as we move forward room to room. When we make it to the kitchen, we'll know that it has a power base there... a concentration. Take it out, snatch Banner, and move it back here and off planet. Then we make the call and have the facility neutralized. Agreed?"

Gage looked at each of them in turn. Riggs sniffled and nodded. McKay, who looked as ready to piss himself as he was to go on a rescue mission, nodded as he clutched the extinguisher to his chest. David nodded as well, but had a hand firmly clamped on the bite. Gage took note. Finally, he turned to Vasquez. She stared off at a wall with her hand on her head. She was a bit pale.

"Vasquez, you get all that?" Gage asked.

Vasquez snapped her head around and winced. She moved her hand from the side of her head to show the damage done to her ear. "Yeah, boss, just trying to shake this off."

Riggs snorted. "She wouldn't let me dress the wound."

Vasquez sneered. "I didn't want to get a staph infection from you after surviving that."

Gage, McKay, and David hid smiles. Gage stepped forward, hands out. "All right, all right. Vasquez, let McKay patch that up before we head out."

"Roger," she said, still sneering at Riggs.

"Good," Gage said taking a deep breath. "We are alpha in five."

Gage left the others to prepare on their own. All he was really concerned with was getting Banner back. She was his rock. Nothing romantic; not in the traditional sense anyways. He fought back a tear thinking of her at the mercy of this thing. She was his moral compass, a full partner in this business and in his life, and he couldn't imagine moving on without her.

Lost in thought, Gage didn't notice David approach until

the younger man cleared his throat. Gage looked up and smiled.

"Hey."

"Hey, Captain. Got a minute?"

Gage nodded, and David swung around to face his brother. "I wanted to say something before we go out there."

"I figured as much."

"I don't blame you for Mom and Dad, anymore."

Gage nodded. "I understand why you did. Lot to resent. I didn't know much about being a role model."

David laughed. "That would explain the strippers at my 14th birthday."

Gage shook his head and smiled. "Those weren't for you; I forgot it was your birthday."

David and Gage laughed together for a moment. It petered out naturally as these things do. They sat for a moment, regarding one another.

"I regret that day," Gage said.

"I regret a lot," David answered. "We might not make it out of this."

Gage nodded. They looked at one another at that point and a multitude of things passed between them. A lot of years were buried for the sake of the next few hours.

"I love you, bro."

David stood and smiled. "I know."

"Make sure Rylene knows her daddy loves her."

"Uncle David is on the case."

Gage grabbed his brother around the shoulders in an embrace that caused David to howl in pain. The younger man jerked back and grasped his damaged arm.

"Slow down on the affection, Captain, walking wounded here." David managed to work up a weak smile between grimaces.

Gage eyed his brother. "I thought it was just a bite.

Before David could answer, Vasquez barked from across the room. "We are alpha, people!"

David smiled and shook it off and wrapped an arm around his brother. "I got this. We got this."

Gage returned the embrace, careful to avoid the shoulder, and they headed toward the entrance to the hallway. Gage was in front with McKay next to him. David and Riggs took the middle, and Vasquez had her tail spot. They headed into the hallway.

CHAPTER TEN

Banner came in and out of consciousness. Her nerves were alive, each of them singing in a hellish harmony. The relay and exo-suit precision melding had gone swimmingly, and as they began to work on the inside of her thigh on the first leg, she had passed out. For the remainder of the process, Banner would come to, smell herself cooking, feel a blinding flash of pain that would cause her vision to swim, and pass out again. Lather, rinse, repeat.

The last time she came around, it wasn't accompanied by the sizzle and shock of a grafter. She was in immense pain, but it was an ache. Post-operative. Despite the situation, Banner smiled. The worst was over. She felt... heavier. What little movement she had told Banner that the exo-suit was in place and relayed. She looked down, forcing her chin as far to her chest as it would go but could only catch glimpses of metal and components.

Her revelations were short lived as Rizzowski and the woman shambled into the room. The glittering sheen that Banner knew was the organism still glinted in the harsh lights. Between the two of them they were carrying a large stock pot used to make large amounts of soup. They stopped in front of Banner and set the pot down on the floor at her feet. She could not see the contents of the pot, but she could hear them, and that caused the bile to rise in her throat.

From the floor near her feet the contents of the pot folded in on itself, over and over. Like a gelatinous mass roiling together, Banner heard the thing in the pot slop and flop around as if it were excited to be there. She was smart and realized that it was excited. It had found a brand new home complete with exo-suit and relays that would give it complete control.

Not for the first time, Banner strained to look to her right. On the very edge of her vision was the door to the kitchen. She knew that any moment Gage would burst through there and take these things out. That's how it always happened. Either she kicked down the door or Gage did… it didn't matter. In their line of work, that had to be the outcome.

Banner squealed as something wet touched her calf. She looked forward and into the face of Rizzowski. He was emotionless, of course. The organism covered his face, condensation dripping from the excessive humidity. There was no joy. No excitement. He was just a drone and the real boss, the real danger slid up the side of Banner's leg.

The woman leaned in and adjusted components on the exo-suit. Soon after, a hum filled the room. Banner equated it to the sound of a ship powering up, warming. Immediately after, her nerve endings changed the song. It was still a harmony, but it didn't ache… there was no pain. It was the tactile equivalent of that hum. Banner felt as if she were 'on.' The switch had been flipped.

Still unable to move, she looked toward the door again.

Gage?

Please?

The organism had spread and was running up the other leg, too. It flowed over the exo-gear and the relays. It spun around her massive thighs, taking its time like some kind of lover, before it flowed in and around her vagina, and over the abs that it had appreciated second-hand with Rizzowski before.

Banner suppressed a squeal and pled with her mind, her heart, and her soul for Gage to come through that door. In the nick of time, now more than ever, she needed her best friend. Her partner.

The hum resonated throughout the room, reverberating off the metal of the kitchen appliances. It echoed in her ears and shook her core. Still, Banner stared at the door. Even as the mass moved over her breasts and neck, inching to her nose and mouth, all she thought of was Gage.

"Damn it," she whispered right before the organism flowed in her nose and mouth. She lurched against her bounds, gagging on the mass.

The last thing that Banner saw before losing consciousness was that closed kitchen door.

After that, there wasn't much Banner left at all.

CHAPTER ELEVEN

It didn't take long before the team made it to the control room and moved toward the corridor that led to the kitchen area. They moved as quietly as possible and didn't encounter any resistance. Gage, leading the group, felt that was odd— but the whole damn job was odd. They continued to move forward until they felt the dripping humidity of the kitchen area.

It had been growing, the heat and moisture, little by little as they moved. Once the group turned a corner that brought them within thirty meters of the environmentally jacked up area, the humidity and temperature smacked them in the face and brought the group to a halt.

"Jesus Christ," David said as he sucked in the heavy air. Everyone else labored to breathe.

Especially Riggs. The small man struggled to catch his breath, the wheezing growing louder and louder. Not one for personal health or hygiene, he was perpetually suffering from some upper respiratory disease or another.

He sneezed.

It was loud and reverberated from wall to wall. The team turned on Riggs, staring him down as the sneeze echoed. Riggs looked up, terrified.

"Oh God... Oh God, I'm sorry!" he said.

No sooner did he get that out when he sneezed again. This was loud, too, but succeeded in spraying a gout of mucus on David. He glared at Riggs as he tried to shake it off.

"Idiot," David whispered.

Riggs turned to apologize when Gage held up a hand, silencing them.

Gage leaned forward toward the end of the hallway and the entrance to the kitchen. He could hear, faintly, a rumbling. He wasn't sure if was a landing ship, an earthquake, or what.

Vasquez bent and felt the floor. She whistled. "Jesus Christ..." she said and looked up.

Gage's eyes went wide, and before he could warn the team, the double doors to the kitchen burst open and were ripped off the hinges.

Through the doorway poured the entire complement of surviving workers and technicians in the building. Gage lost count at twenty, and then they were on the team. Gage fired first, catching one of the assailants in the neck, ripping the side of the man's neck apart, and cauterizing the wound all in the same blast. The man spun backwards but managed to use the momentum follow through and continue forward. Gage fired again, this time taking the top of the man's head off. He dropped to the ground, losing all motivation.

David fired and Vasquez pumped round after round, taking a couple of lab-coated assailants out before the mass was too close and too thick to fire. They fought tooth and nail and hand to hand.

McKay and Riggs actually developed a system that was particularly effective. Riggs would douse one of the compromised assailants with cold extinguisher, slowing the person down. As the assailant dropped to their knees or slumped against a wall, McKay would swing his extinguisher at his or her head. There was enough weight that the skull would crack, sending shards of bone into the brain. This, then, allowed the organism nothing to control. The pair would then switch on the next attacker. Both Riggs and McKay retched at first after each shot and attempted to wipe the brain matter, fragments, and blood from the canisters, but the press became too thick. The pair of science specialists then reacted on instinct, trusting one another intuitively. The sound of the spray, the crack of metal on skull, and the thump of a body on the floor played out like a drum line.

David and Vasquez fought with everything they had. Vasquez positioned herself in front of David's damaged arm, protecting his side and hiding her damaged ear at the same time. She had the baton out and the rifle was slung around her shoulder so smoothly that David did not see it happen.

Vasquez would lash out quickly with the baton, either taking shots to the head of the horde or pushing the end of the baton, the thinner end, right through the assailant's eye socket and into the brain. Each time she pushed that baton forward into the eye itself, severing the optic nerve and pressing into the soft membranes that announced the cerebral cortex, the duo lost precious time as she used her foot to force the skewered attacker off the baton and on the floor.

Each time she did that, the sound reminded David of a family vacation from years before. He knew it was ridiculous, faced with life and death, to remember his brother sucking down oysters somewhere on the East Coast of America, making him cringe at the sound as a young boy. As he lashed out with the butt of the plasma gun, bringing it down over and over again trying to ram it through the skulls of the parasite-infested men and women that were trying to kill him, he found solace in the memory.

Only Gage fought alone. At the front of the team he took the first of the horde as they spilled over him. He abandoned the pistol quickly, right after the first kill, and went with his bare hands. He fought furiously, only thinking that it didn't matter how many of these things he had to go through, he would get to Banner.

Gage grabbed a former scientist by the sides of the head and sunk his thumbs into the thing's eye sockets. It struggled for a moment, beating against Gage's arms, but he pressed further. The tension finally gave way, and he managed to get his thumbs through and into the brain tissue. With a snarl, he tossed the corpse aside and went for the next one. This person used to be a chef or dish washer or someone working in the kitchen. He grabbed the woman's head, and with a scream, forced that head into the tiled floor. Again and again, he rammed the woman's skull into the floor, only stopping when that head split like a melon, spilling the its contents onto the tile.

Gage stood and roared at those remaining, spit and sweat flying from his mouth and brow. Despite their mindless state, the ten or so remaining assailants stopped short.

"Banner!" Gage yelled into heat and moisture and darkness.

The horde gathered again and moved forward, and Gage tore into them, rending with his hands and feet. His one goal was to get to Banner, and nothing living or dead or in between would stop him.

The team fought forward valiantly, taking each of these things down one at time. They inched closer into the kitchen, taking ground from the enemy measured in fractions. Vasquez skewered, David bashed, Riggs and McKay went through assailants with their version of the one-two punch. Gage, alone taking point, continued to fight and rip and tear.

Vasquez pushed a janitor off of her baton with her foot and looked up for the first time in what seemed like an hour and saw no one in front of her. David, his breath coming in heaving gasps, drove the butt of the pistol through the head of another person for the last time, and that attacker dropped.

Riggs and McKay finished with their last assailant while Gage, without an opponent, looked from side to side like a feral animal expecting to be attacked at any moment.

The quiet, aside from the labored breathing from the team, was oppressive. No moans, no grunts. The sounds of skulls being compromised or painful wailings from the team, so commonplace before, left a void in their absence. This silence was interrupted, quietly at first, from something inside the darkened kitchen area. It was quiet at first, like a faint click, click, click… metal on metal. As the sound grew louder, the team unconsciously pulled together.

Vasquez and David continued to protect each other's weaknesses while McKay and Riggs slipped in front of them, going to the middle. Only Gage stayed out front, ready for anything, but desperately hoping that Banner would rush out and great them.

As the shape in the darkness took form, the team was speechless. Gage got his wish and immediately regretted it.

All the weapons dropped, and the team could only stare straight ahead.

David broke the silence. "Jesus Christ."

Standing before them was Banner 2.0. She was nude, but the exo-suit had been soldered to her body. The mechanical unit ran up both sides of her leg and ended in metal boots. He pelvic area and abdomen were covered in the same metal, and it was scaled, like armor, to be flexible. Her arms resembled the legs, and her upper torso was also scaled like her abdomen. The point of the exo-suit was to accent the natural strength and speed of the wearer as it bonded with the organism. This suit was bonded to Banner herself, and the organism inhabited her. There was no telling what she could do.

Banner's head was ensconced in the same scaled metal like a helmet. Protruding from the exo-suit, and buried deep in her skin, were the filament-like relays that allowed the nervous system to respond to the suit and vice versa. Hundreds of the relays sprung from all over her body and sizzled with energy. Her body was covered in that glistening sheen that indicated that the organism was in control. She smiled, but it was cold; humorless.

"David Gage," she said. It was throaty and obviously uncomfortable to her to speak. It was Banner's voice, of course, but it sounded as if she hadn't said anything for a very long time, and the words were foreign. "We are aware of this Jesus, and do not believe He will be able to save you."

At that point, the massive bio-mechanical organism that used to be Banner laughed. It sounded like an old man with a wheezing cough, and the team shrunk back when they heard it.

Except for Gage. Gage stood there, facing the thing, and held back tears.

CHAPTER TWELVE

Banner raised her hand, the mechanics humming along and the relays sizzling. "We have no desire to harm you. We require your ship, that is all."

Riggs nodded. "I knew it! She wants off the planet."

"Correct."

"You made sure that it was our ship that came, didn't you?" McKay asked.

Banner nodded.

Gage glared up at the thing. Normally, Banner had a few inches on him, but with the addition of the exo-suit, this version of Banner was closer to a full foot taller. "You wanted Banner."

She smiled and opened her arms wide, the exo-suit responding. "Very perceptive."

David stepped up and around McKay and Riggs. He joined his brother. "We are going to stop you and rip you the hell out of Banner."

"We think not." Banner's eyes closed.

Vasquez screamed. The team spun to see her grab her head in immense pain. The bandage that covered her damaged ear pulsed and pressed. Something underneath that bandage pushed outwards, stretching the bandage to its limit.

Vasquez fell backwards and tore at the bandage, ripping it free. From within her ear a translucent tendril, a familiar sight with this group, shot outward from her ear and wrapped itself the side of her face. Vasquez' eyes glazed over, and she stopped screaming.

Gage turned to Banner. "Let her go!"

Banner chuckled. Gage turned back to see Vasquez slip the rifle from her shoulder. Before anyone could move she had the weapon up and discharged. At such a close range, Riggs' head nearly disintegrated before their eyes.

His corpse dropped to the floor. Vasquez shifted, setting her sights on David.

McKay screamed and blasted Vasquez in the face with the cold extinguisher. She dropped to her knees, and the tendril shot out from her ear again, trying to escape the temperature drop. McKay, distraught at the death of his friend, raised the canister in the air. David caught him in time before he could bring it crashing down on Vasquez' head. Gage stepped forward and grabbed the tendril as it flailed. He pulled, sliding it from Vasquez' ear. At full length it was nearly four feet long and the diameter of thick rope.

Eyes rimmed with tears, McKay stared at it. It wriggled and fought, weakly trying to get into Gage. He turned from Vasquez to the thing, unsure where to place his rage.

David leaned into McKay. "Hasan. There, that's the real villain."

McKay sneered. He nodded to Gage. With a real effort, Gage shook the thing off, and it hit the floor with a splat. Before it could get anywhere, McKay stepped on what could have either been a head or a tail, but the science officer knew it was neither.

"This is for Riggs," he said, and aimed the extinguisher at it. He blasted the thing until the tank was empty. When the chemical cloud cleared, the tendril was frozen solid. McKay lifted his foot and stomped on the thing, shattering it like ice.

David helped Vasquez up. She held her hand to the side of her face. She was barely conscious.

"Unfortunate," Banner said.

Crying out, McKay stepped forward before Gage could catch him and attacked Banner, swinging the empty extinguisher in a wide arc. Faster than anyone could believe, Banner blocked the attack with her arm, the metal clanging off one another. Without hesitating, she kicked McKay in the chest, and he flew backwards like he weighed next to nothing. He slammed into the far wall, hitting his head and nearly losing consciousness.

David, holding Vasquez up, stared at Banner. He was joined by Gage. Banner stepped forward, set on taking care of them and using the ship to escape.

Gage turned to his brother. "Go. Get them to the ship."

David shook his head. He knew that look his brother had. He had seen it once before when he told David their parents had died. "Andy... no." Vasquez shifted, and David turned to her, repositioning himself and trying to keep her upright.

"Get to the ship."

"Tell them I love them."

Gage nodded and turned to Banner. His eyes narrowed, and he raised his weapon. "There is no way you're getting to that ship."

Banner laughed that same grating sound.

Gage glanced over his shoulder to make sure that the team was gone. David had done his job; they were moving as fast as they could down the hallway. He turned back to the thing that used to be his best friend.

"I love you, Banner."

"If she were here, she would probably respond in kind." Banner stepped forward, quickly.

Gage side-stepped, narrowly missing being decapitated by a swipe if the cyborg's exo-suit gloved hand. The speed was tremendous, and he nearly lost his footing from the force of the blow passing in front of him. Regardless, Gage fired a plasma bolt. It struck Banner on the left arm. The exo-suit deflected a large part of it, but Gage could see the organism's shiny over-skin sizzling. The relays around the damaged organism crackled with energy, and before Gage's very eyes, the thing repaired itself. He stepped back, eyes wide.

"It is in your best interest, Andrew Gage, to allow us access to your ship."

Gage smiled. Every clichéd line from every good vs. evil story rushed through his mind. He could only manage a whispered, "Hang tight, Banner, here I come."

With that, Gage bellowed at the metal and flesh and bone and parasite patchwork creature in front of him and rushed forward.

He didn't make it far. With a strangled cry, Gage was scooped up, both of Banner's clad hands wrapped around his neck. She lifted him up so that they were face to face.

"We recognize the attachment you have with our host, and as a start to socialization, we will allow you to die as you gaze upon her."

With that, the organism slid down Banner's face. The glossy sheen disappeared, allowing a small oval of Banner, and nothing else to fill Gage's vision.

Gage kicked and struggled and gagged and sucked in as much air as he could. Banner's hands tightened quickly. She could have probably torn his head off before the suit and the pressure mounted.

Tears ran down Gage's face. He refused to look away from that small oval. That little bit of Banner that he could hold onto in his final moments. Before his larynx was crushed, he managed to croak out a final question. "Banner... is there any of you left in there?"

Banner squeezed, her fingers digging in. Each side of Gage's neck exploded in a shower of blood as the carotid arteries fell prey to the crushing power of Banner.

Gage's eyes fluttered. Oxygen deprivation, loss of blood, and the pain from being mid-way through a severed spine had taken their toll. He was rapidly losing consciousness. Before he succumbed to his injuries, Banner brought him nose to nose and decided to answer his question.

"No."

Gage's eyes rolled into the back of his head just as Banner's hands met in the middle of his neck. Gage's headless body dropped to the floor.

Banner continued to hold Gage's head up as the shiny sheen of the organism once again covered her face. She looked at the head, and if the organism had anything akin to human emotion, she would have frowned.

She tossed the head to the side and stepped forward and down the hallway, heading straight for the docking bay.

CHAPTER THIRTEEN

David, Vasquez, and Hasan burst into the docking area. They stumble around the bodies, trying to make it to the ship's door. Vasquez had recovered a bit and was helping, but the going was slow. McKay followed behind the duo, his brow knit.

David leaned Vasquez against a wall and scanned the room, looking for anything they could use as a weapon. He spotted the survival suits and grabbed three. He turned to hand them out to the crew and saw McKay standing before Vasquez. He just stood there staring. The look on his face was pure menace. Quickly, David stepped between McKay and Vasquez, breaking the science officer's concentration.

"Get it under control, Hasan."

"She killed Riggs!"

Vasquez looked up at that. Tears rimmed her eyes.

"No she didn't, man… think about it."

Hasan screamed. He threw the extinguisher canister he was holding across the room and snarled. "God damn it!"

David handed Hasan a suit and put his hand on the taller man's shoulder. "That thing killed Riggs. It killed Banner, and I'm sure it killed Andy. OK? Get a hold of yourself, and get suited up."

McKay went to argue but gave up. With a deep breath he turned away from Vasquez and started putting the suit on.

David handed Vasquez a suit. She grabbed his shirt before he could move.

"I killed Riggs, he's right…" Vasquez choked on the words. David had never seen her so messed up.

"Bull shit. It was that thing. We'll talk about it when we're a few thousand miles away, all right?"

Vasquez nodded. She dropped the rifle to the floor and started suiting up as well.

David scanned the room. They had already taken the weapons and the extinguishers for the hallway assault. He didn't know what he was looking for, but he hoped he would find it soon.

Hasan kept an eye on the hallway. There was no sign of anything coming their way just yet, but he stayed vigilant. Over his shoulder he called to David.

"Do you have the code?"

David looked up. "What code?"

Hasan exchanged a glance with Vasquez. She hung her head before looking up. "The access code to the ship. We can get in with a bio scan, Banner, or Gage's code. Other than that, we're screwed."

David, panicking, looked around the room even more frantically than before. Hasan split his gaze from the hallway to David. Vasquez looked to David, too. He stopped and slumped against the wall.

"I don't know."

"What do you mean you don't know? How can you not have a plan?" Hasan screamed. He turned his back on the hallway and walked into the bay area. His anger flared.

Vasquez struggled to a standing position and pulled the

rifle out as McKay advanced on David. Hasan turned to her. A full two feet taller than the security officer, his nature belied his size. This was the first time anyone had seen McKay in this state.

"Back down," Vasquez ordered, aiming the rifle at McKay.

"Or, what? You going to kill me like you killed Riggs!"

"You think I wanted to do that? Is that what your think?!"

David watched the two of them step closer, inching to a violent resolution. It couldn't end like this. He flew off the wall and stepped between the two of them. David batted the rifle down, and he pushed McKay back. The taller man stumbled toward the hallway; he turned and glared.

"Enough," David said. "I am not Andy. I'm not a leader, but we have to think through this. We are the only ones standing between that thing and a populated planet. A real populated planet, not some ball of ice in the middle of nowhe…"

David's voice trailed off and he looked to Hasan. McKay caught the drift of the idea and nodded.

"Think it can work?" David asked.

"What can work?" Vasquez had no idea what they were talking about.

"Yeah, if the suits hold up." McKay looked up, making a few calculations in his head. "We'll need a good ninety seconds."

David nodded. He turned to Vasquez, ready convey the concept of how they were going to stop Banner and get off planet, when the entrance to the docking bay from the hallway filled with the hulking form of their nemesis herself. David noticed right away that her hands were covered in blood. His brother's blood. He took a deep breath.

Hasan turned to find Banner inches from him. He knew

this was it, there was no way to outrun the woman before enhancements... and now? He smiled, coughed as hard as he could, and spit a glob of mucus the size of a grape into the face of his former supervisor.

"That was for Riggs," he said. That would have made his friend proud.

David took the time Hasan had bought them with the theatrics to lean into Vasquez. "Suit up fast, and when I give the order, fire everything you got into her. Got it?"

Vasquez smiled and hefted the rifle. "Yes, sir."

David pulled the survival suit over his head just in time to see Banner eviscerate McKay.

One swipe of the hand, and she nearly sliced the man in half. He stood there for a moment, watching his intestines, liver, and viscera fall to the ground. McKay made a half-hearted attempt to collect it with his hands, but eventually, he followed the organs to the ground.

David inched toward the panel for the door and tapped at it, working the default codes. Banner looked from Vasquez to Banner and put the plan together pretty quickly.

"Fire!" David yelled out.

Vasquez took a quick second to finish connecting the suit so it was insulated and brought the rifle up to her shoulder. She fired into Banner, knocking her back a foot.

Banner stepped forward, the relays crackling, and the organism sizzling. As fast as it repaired itself, Vasquez got off another shot. A foot back, a long stride forward. Vasquez fired again and again, impeding the thing's progress but not stopping it. Blast, sizzling organism, blast, sizzling organism.

Surprisingly, Banner ignored Vasquez and focused on David. She realized where the real danger was. Shrugging off the plasma rifle was no mean feat, and it took everything, but she inched toward David.

For his part, David frantically punched code after code

into the panel. Every cheater, default, company-sponsored safe code… whatever he could remember.

Banner got closer and closer. A final shot rang out, knocking her back right before she reached David.

"I'm out!" Vasquez yelled.

Banner laughed, that grating sound again. "Like your brother." She cackled again and reached out for David.

The panel flashed green and David dropped to his ass, sitting on the floor to avoid the grasping arms of the creature in front of him. He looked up at the thing that used to be Banner. The thing that killed his teammates and his brother. David grinned from ear to ear.

"Enjoy the weather."

David hit enter and the door to the exterior slid open. Even through the survival suits, David and Vasquez could feel the cutting wind. Nearly nude and covered in metal, Banner didn't stand much of chance.

She backed up, trying to get to the safety of the humidity controlled kitchen, but the blast of frigid air stopped her in her tracks. A negative thirty temp was only a precursor, the foundation for a wind chill that froze Banner in her tracks.

As David and Vasquez watched, the organism panicked and revolted. Tendrils desperately pulled away from the relays and the exo-suit, but the blast of sub-freezing weather was simply far too much. It only took a few moments for Centauri Six to reduce Banner to a veritable ice statue, one hand in the air and the other trying to block the wind. She froze with her mouth open and eyes wide. Terrified.

David smiled. Good. He was glad they could teach the thing a human emotion. He looked to Vasquez and pointed to his wrist. They didn't have much time. The survival suits were not a permanent solution to this planet's surface.

Vasquez nodded. She hefted the rifle by its barrel and turned to Banner. Hoisting the rifle like a bat, she swung at the creature's outstretched arm. The heavy rifle stock connected with the arm, snapping it off at the elbow.

David caught the arm before it could hit the floor of the bay.

Vasquez tossed the rifle to the side, and they exited the bay door with David holding the key to getting into the ship.

CHAPTER FOURTEEN

Vasquez sat on the edge of the chyro bunk. David walked back from the bridge of the ship. He smiled, wearily. Vasquez managed a weak return. They were already miles off the surface of the planet.

"I think I've got us pointed in the right direction," David said, sitting on the edge of another of the bunks.

Vasquez nodded. She stared at the wall behind David, her eyes welling up. "I don't want to think about...you know."

David nodded. He looked around the bay and smiled. The place was so uniquely Andy's and Banner's. They lived in the ship... guess that was his now. "He was wrong."

Vasquez looked up. "Gage?"

"I did appreciate him. I really did."

Vasquez smiled. This time she meant it. "He knew. You wouldn't be within twenty light years of this job if he didn't."

David frowned and stood. He shucked off his gear getting down to his underclothes. "Better get in there, we'll be flying for a while."

Vasquez nodded. She started to take off her gear and looked at David while he was prepping his bunk. "Hey, David."

He turned.

"About Riggs..."

David shook his head and held up his hand before she

could go further. "Just get in the chyro. We'll figure it out when we get back planet-side."

David got in the bunk and shut himself in. It took a moment for the bunk to stabilize, but the pod locked down. David watched as Vasquez prepared for the chyro sleep.

Vasquez dropped her gear and uniform, too, and right before she laid down, she felt a small itching sensation on the back of her neck. As she reached back to scratch it, she turned.

David could see from his pod, the smallest patch of glistening… something on the back of Vasquez' neck. His eyes went wide in recognition as he saw the shiny little blob move toward Vasquez' ear. A little tendril, translucent and shimmering under the ship's halogen lighting, disappeared inside the young woman.

He started to scream and scrambled to reach the kill switch in the chyro pod. The unit itself was a fraction of a second quicker, and before he could do anything, the gas dispensed in the pod, and he was out instantly.

Vasquez stood and turned, looking at David's bunk for a moment. With a smile, she stepped forward and toward the bridge of the ship.

POST-CREDIT SEQUENCE!

MODEL EMPLOYEE

Skippy, the stock boy, was lonely. He worked the night shift. Stocking shelves, of course. The D-Mart was dark at night. Dark as pitch, but he worked on. Skippy wasn't like the other stock boys. Or stock girls. Or cashiers. Certainly not like Mrs. Lippman, the manager. Skippy couldn't be seen by customers. He was a little slow. He looked funny, too. His arms were too long. His face was funny. Born with too much forehead, Mrs. Lippman said. Too much forehead was funny. Like an upside-down ice cream cone. Skippy chuckled. He was wearing a white shirt tonight. Vanilla melty ice cream. He was strong, though. Skippy lifted things that other people couldn't. Right up in the air. Laughing, Skippy lifted a tractor up. It belonged in the Garden Department.

Skippy settled the tractor down carefully. He had been too excited once. He broke a snow blower. Mrs. Lippman was mad. She scolded Skippy. He didn't like that. He got so upset, he hurt things. When he had a *moment* stuff got wet. He tried not to, but it happened. So, he was careful. Skippy was funny that way, too. When he got mad he couldn't stop.

He had to grab and squeeze. Anything soft and gushy. He broke the snow blower on accident. Mrs. Lippman knew that, but wouldn't listen. Too bad Ellie worked late. She was pretty. She cleaned the floors. She was nice to Skippy, too. Not like Mrs. Lippman. He was so angry. He grabbed Ellie and squeezed. Melty ice cream was strawberry after that. Mrs. Lippman understood when she came in that morning. She cleaned up. She sent Skippy home (to the garage). Poor Ellie.

Skippy heard a sound and stopped thinking of past stuff. He whipped around, toward the offices. Garden was a whole store away but he heard the sounds. Skippy's ears were funny, too. Really big, like plates. He heard good. He heard people talking by the offices.

Mrs. Lippman said to never go there. The offices were off limits. Skippy didn't want to make her mad. Not again. But there were people! He heard them. Skippy bounded forward. He leapt from spot to spot. He made it across the whole store. Only three jumps this time. A new record.

Two men, dressed in black jammed a metal bar in the door crack. The door popped open. To Skippy, it sounded weird. Like dropping ravioli cans. He loved ravioli. That was all he ate.

The men went in the office. Skippy sprang up. He knew Mrs. Lippman would yell. He knew she would blame him. Two men? In black clothes? No way, she was too tough. He felt himself getting angry.

His face heated up. That is how it started. The hair on his back tingled. The too much forehead got hot. Right to the tippy top. Skippy's piggy eyes smoldered. Mrs. Lippman called them piggy eyes. He liked that. Sometimes he would snort like a pig. Mrs. Lippman smiled then, too. But not now. Now he was too angry to snort.

Skippy could feel the want. The gushy, wet want. Those

men were bad. They would get him in trouble. Mrs. Lippman would yell. And yell. Loud. Mean. Hateful things.

The two men exited the office, smiling. One of them held a large bag. Skippy didn't care who they were. No way.

Skippy vaulted over the rack of lingerie. He landed in front of the men. They turned, startled, smiles dropped. Skippy stood before them. The name tag said so. Muscles rippled underneath the white shirt. Skippy's eyes glossed over, rationality gone. A snarl creased his face. His red face. Beat red to the top of the cone head.

The men dropped the bag. Before they could make a peep, even. Skippy reached up. He took a head in each massive hand. Skippy squeezed. His fingers dug into their skulls. Eyes popped divots. Not content, Skippy pushed in. Yes, he squeezed their skulls. The red stuff, and gray stuff. The men shook. They rattled. They jitterbugged. All the while, Skippy squeezed.

He squeezed until the mad went away. How long? He didn't know. Long enough. The men stopped shaking. They hung in the air. Skippy's breathing calmed down. His head cooled, starting at the top. The heat dissipated, passing his cheeks. Skippy's back hair lay flat. He calmed.

Skippy used his foot. The men wouldn't shake off his fingers. He had to push them off. Skippy smiled.

Mrs. Lippman would be happy. He could prove he didn't go in there. Not in the office. Never.

Skippy wiped his hands on his shirt. He went back to Garden. More tractors to move. Always more work.

ABOUT THE AUTHOR

David C. Hayes is an author, performer and filmmaker. His films, like *A Man Called Nereus, Dark Places* and *The Frankenstein Syndrome* (and approximately 70 more) can be seen worldwide. He is the writer of *Rottentail*, the feature film based off his graphic novel of the same name. His comic book mini-series, *The Rot*, has debuted to acclaim. He is the author of several novels, collections, chapbooks and graphic novels including *Cherub, Knight Chills, Cannibal Fat Camp, Pegged, American Guignol* and *Muddled Mind: The Complete Works of Ed Wood, Jr.* As a playwright, David's full-length and one-act plays have been produced from coast to coast with a run Off-Broadway for the comedy *Swamp Ho* and sell-out performances in Phoenix for *Dial P for Peanuts* (winning a 2011 Ethingtony for Best Show).

DRAGON'S ROOST PRESS

Dragon's Roost Press is the fever dream brainchild of dark speculative fiction author Michael Cieslak. Since 2014, their goal has been to find the best speculative fiction authors and share their work with the public. For more information about Dragon's Roost Press and their publications, please visit:

http://thedragonsroost.net/styled-3/index.html.

ALSO AVAILABLE FROM
DRAGON'S ROOST PRESS

Edited by Michael Cieslak   Edited by Michael Cieslak

C ryptozoology -- "the study of hidden animals"
    The search for and study of animals whose exis-
tence or survival is disputed or unsubstantiated

MENAGERIE: A STRANGE OR DIVERSE COLLECTION OF people or things.

WELCOME TO THE HIDDEN MENAGERIE -- TWO collections of short fiction involving various cryptozoological creatures. In the first volume you will meet the beasts of the land. Inside these pages you will be introduced to new visions of some creatures you are familiar with like the Abominable Snowman and the Wendigo. In the second, the beasts of the air, sea, and animate vegetation — the Kraken, Mermaids, and Lake Monsters. Both volumes contain creatures long thought extinct which live on to this day, and others you may have never heard of. creatures long thought extinct which live on to this day, and others you may have never heard of.

Combine the mind splintering horror of the Cthulhu Mythos and the heart shattering portion of that most terrible of emotions - love - and what do you have? You have Eldritch Embraces: Putting the Love Back in Lovecraft. This collection of short stories from some of the best working in the fields of horror and dark speculative fiction blends romance and Lovecraft in a way which will may make you sigh, smile, weep, or leave you the hollow shell of your former self.

Robotic Animals, Televisions Which Reveal Alternate Universes, Inanimate Objects Brought to Life, People Struggling to Survive in Apocalyptic Wastelands, Sentient Cutlery, and much, much more.

Desolation: 21 Tales for Tails is a collection of dark speculative fiction whose stories all focus on themes of loneliness, isolation, and abandonment. Enter into strange worlds envisioned by some of the most inventive authors writing today. A portion of the proceeds of each sale of Desolation: 21 Tales for Tails benefits the Last Day Dog Rescue Organization.

JERICHO RISING

Mary Lynne Gibbs

In post-World War III, small town Michigan, a self-proclaimed, violent, and insane High Priestess has taken control, reducing the remaining men to nothing more than slaves and play-things. Jericho, the reluctant leader of the Resistance, must fight her own family to preserve the freedom and equality of all in her care - male and female alike. She's torn between love and duty, and with traitors around every corner, she has no idea who to trust anymore.

JERICHO'S
REDEMPTION

MARY LYNNE GIBBS

The battle is over, but the war has just begun. Jericho returns to the Obsidian camp, only to learn that her sister Candace destroyed it as part of a plot to dismantle the resistance movement that brought down their mother, the High Priestess. The rest of the resistance blames Jericho for the deaths of their friends, but that's the least of her worries. Not only does Jericho now have to right the wrongs her sister has done, she must contend with a few guests to the camp who bring secrets that will change her life forever. Either she'll redeem herself in the eyes of her comrades, or she'll die trying.

The best man on the pirate ship is a girl named Alex.

ALEXANDRA "ALEX" GARDNER IS THE RELUCTANT CABIN boy on The Bloody Maiden, a ruthless pirate ship run by the charmingly evil Captain Montgomery. The crew is convinced she's a boy, and she hopes it stays that way until she has the chance to avenge the deaths of her mother and brother at the hands of the crew. All goes well until the ship takes a handsome captive. Could her feelings for him ruin her charade?

SEBASTIAN WHITLEY IS A YOUNG MAN IN LOVE. HE SAILS on his father's ship, trying to find the beautiful girl he's lost. When he's captured by The Bloody Maiden, the annoying cabin boy saves his life – and makes it more difficult at the same time. His savior is actually a girl, and if Sebastian doesn't keep quiet, it could mean both their deaths. Together, they have to thwart a mutiny, get revenge, and get off the ship before Alex's secret is revealed. If not, it's the plank for both of them.

Ever wonder how you might handle a sabbatical from work? Think the bible told you everything there is to know about the Devil? What if the noises coming from under your child's bed weren't just in his imagination? Crack open Hell Hath No Fury, a collection of 21 tales of horror and dark fiction, to learn the answers to these questions. Discover stories of psychotic delusions, ghosts, a murder victim's revenge, and a family brought closer together through torture. All of this and more awaits inside this collection of stories from horror master Peggy Christie.

Do you enjoy creepy stories about people who don't quite fit in? Dead Girls Don't Love is a collection of poignant tales for the outsider in all of us.

FOR A DOMESTIC VIOLENCE VICTIM, THERE IS NO LIFE after death--but could there be revenge?

Can a woman returning to her life after 40 years with the fae remember how to be human?

When two Buddhist monks travel to China to spread the dharma, will they survive the unspeakable horror they find instead?

What really happened when the Big Bad Wolf ate the lonely grandmother living in the woods?

Will the love between two zombified women help them break the spell that binds them in eternal servitude?

And, perhaps most importantly, can an Elder God find true love?

THESE AND MANY MORE FASCINATING QUESTIONS WILL be answered on the pages within, if you dare to read them. But be warned: the strange and horrifying realities contained in Dead Girls Don't Love may haunt you long after you close the back cover.

Not long ago, Zuzanna Uritski was a cleaner at the 1893 Chicago World's Fair, Archibald Campion was the Fair's most imaginative engineer, and Elspeth was a lifeless automaton. But now? Now they're demon hunters, pursuing an ancient evil that has traveled across universes to take residence in one of history's most famous serial killers. Travel to an alternate history where no one is safe from demon possession, automatons are self-aware, and the world's greatest hope lies with a clever engineer, a dauntless young woman, and a paladin from another world.

Wait! Seriously, hang on a minute before opening this book. In case the title, and lurid, disturbing image on the front haven't already made it shockingly clear, THIS BOOK IS NOT FOR CHILDREN. Or people with sensitive stomachs. Or taste.

ENTER THE TWISTED MIND OF HORROR AUTHOR KEN MacGregor as he explores the boundaries of horror, eroticism, and yes, taste.